SANDY DUNES RESORT

Happy reading!

SANDY DUNES RESORT

JOANN BUIE

Copyright © 2023 by Joann Buie

Independently published by Desert Wind Press LLC
www.desertwindpress.com

ISBN 978-1-956271-16-4 (paperback)
ISBN 978-1-956271-17-1 (ebook)

Contents

𝒫ROLOGUE

I grew up spending most of my life at my Aunt Sandy's Resort in Michigan. After my mom had died when I was eight years old, Aunt Sandy took the responsibility of raising me until I went to college. I finished college getting a Business Degree, and decided to stay in New York City where I had landed a job working in a private banking establishment.

I was engaged to my boss, the owner of the bank, working tedious hours on projects after projects for him. I thought he was the greatest thing at the time, then I was proven wrong, and my engagement was off.

That made the second love of my life fall short of marriage. Tommy was my first love at the resort when we were teenagers, but when I went off to college I didn't hear from him again. I sent letters daily to him receiving nothing back. After graduation from college, I stopped hoping to hear from him, and went on with my life. That was when I met Phillip and was hired at his bank. Tommy was then out of the picture, and replaced with Phillip.

Phillip wasn't the wonderful man as I thought he was and when I found that out about him, I was fired immediately from the bank. I had no other place to go but back home to Aunt Sandy, and was worried I wouldn't get back home before another rotten thing would happened. My safety was in jeopardy now, and I knew somehow or another I had to get away from Phillip finding me, before I could safely leave.

Not only was I taking a chance of Phillip locating me, I was also in part, knowing information of fraud, and not letting the proper authorities know about the crime Phillip had been doing for so long. I knew what he was capable of doing to keep that a secret, no matter what the cost was. That was the part that terrified me the most.

When I got home it felt good, but Phillip wasn't completely out of the picture by a long shot. Many times I had to look over my shoulder in fear that he would some how be stocking me.

I felt as if I was a failure in life now. Failed at two loves, failed at a fantastic job that I was fired from, scared out of my wits regarding my safety, and having to move back home feeling like a loser, shamed, and embarrassed.

With Aunt Sandy's help and understanding, and the help I received from others, I was able to overcome the hellish nightmare that happened in New York City. Being able to tell my story I feel that I have gotten justice for other people wronged at the bank, and feel vindicated for what Phillip had made me go through. The truth will set you free, and it did for me!

$\mathcal{J}$ULY

I fly home to Michigan every summer to visit my Aunt Sandy, at her resort on Lake Huron. She was the one who raised me after my mother had passed away, when I was eight years old. That was the worse day of my life, but Aunt Sandy assured me we would always remember my mom. I lost my mom, and she had lost her sister, who was also her best friend. We were going to move on with our lives together helping each other along the way.

My mom had been an elementary school teacher most of her life, and her illness came on quickly taking her life about as fast. It was the hardest thing I had to deal with in my life. My dad wasn't in the picture at all, but I knew his name, and it was just that, a name to me, nothing more, nothing less. My mom told me he didn't want to be a father, to be tied down with responsibilities, and bolted when my mother told him she was pregnant. So, I wasn't planned and he definitely didn't want to be a father so one night he left the house they had shared together, and left town without warning. I was thankful my mother wanted me, and raised me until she wasn't able to any longer. I felt sad for my mom, when she told me all this, and she vowed she would never trust men again in her life. All I could do is dream of the day I would become a mother, and I knew I wanted to be just like my mom when I did become one.

I think it was something every girl dreams about while growing up, including the important wedding plans that changed every few weeks. I knew what my dream husband would be like, too. Tall, dark, and definitely handsome, like in the books I read whenever I could. He would be the kindest, happiest man that would make lots of money at his job, and love me always and forever.

Aunt Sandy had always wanted children of her own, but she wasn't able to conceive for some odd reason. Her first husband, Darren, had been killed in action during the war, and she had never remarried, until much later in life. I never knew her first husband, my uncle, but he sounded like a wonderful man from what my mom had told me, and very good to my aunt. Aunt Sandy always said we were her family, feeling blessed having us with her was all she needed. She had a heart of gold working herself to the bone making her resort run as smooth as it did, to making herself a few extra dollars.

My mom and I would spend our entire summers with her at her resort, located on the sandy shores of Lake Huron, as soon as school was out. When I got off the school bus, mom had the car already packed with our clothes, and snacks for me, just waiting for me to hop in the car so we could leave.

She loved the resort as much as I did, and being with her sister.

Mom helped Aunt Sandy every summer, by cleaning the twenty-four cabins after the guests left, and washing the many loads of soiled laundry that was involved. I had never seen a basement that had ten washing machines lining the walls with as many dryers, all in one place, other than at the laundromat. Aunt Sandy's basement was just that, and they were always in use when it came to changing the linens for the next guest to use.

I loved it there, the best part of my life growing up involved the resort. Aunt Sandy never hesitated to take me in to live with her, even before my mom's funeral was over. She was there to comfort me when I needed it, and I'd like to think I was able to help her through mom's passing on some days, too. She knew there were other family members that would try to take me, but Aunt Sandy didn't think they would be a good fit for me, only wanting me for the money they'd receive, and not much on the nurturing side. My mom had it in her will stating this as well, with Aunt Sandy promising her she would care for me. We didn't visit any other family very often, and I always overheard the many conversations mom, and Aunt Sandy had about them. They weren't too fond of the relatives for some reason I never understood.

Sandy's Dunes Resort was always filled with activities to do all summer long, which I was included in on all that I wanted, as if I was a guest there. As I got older, the jet skis and boating became my favorite pass time, using them as much as possible. Nothing like having the lake as your own playground. I had the best backyard that anyone could want.

Tommy was close to my age and my best friend, that was

living at the resort with his grandfather, Thomas. We would be gone for hours on the jet skis when we could escape, and enjoyed every second of it when we were of age to drive them. We both knew our chores came first, and we never complained knowing we would be rewarded with time on the water once we were done.

Having a beach life was my main purpose in life at that time, and I spent every second I could in my preteen and teen years there. I loved the sun and all the water activities. I was also getting the darkest tan possible. It showed everyone at school, when we went back in September, that I was a sun worshiper. Never took any advise about getting too much sun though, or that the sun could damage my skin. I just wanted that dark tan, no matter what it took.

The beach sand was such a soft texture, and the purest white ever seen, that burned the bottom of my feet when I wasn't careful. The bluish green water of Lake Huron was warm, and the nights were cool enough to have several bonfires blazing along the shore. If we didn't have one on our beach, there were plenty others along the coast that a person could join into. I was at a bonfire about every night mingling with the locals, and our guests as well.

When I was in high school, I started working on Aunt Sandy's books showing her several ways to save more money, and items she could take off her taxes as expense, as I learned each trick of the trade in my business class. I knew then what I wanted to do when I went to college, and set my mind to complete college in record time.

Many people expected me to go into the medical field, because of what had happened to my mom, but that wasn't what I wanted. I didn't like being in the hospital when I had to go, and I certainly didn't want it to remind me of my mom's last days alive. I liked the business field. Aunt Sandy understood, and encouraged me to do what I wanted. That was all I needed, her support, and have something that I was really good at doing.

I went home every six months for a week to work on Aunt Sandy's books when I went away to college. It was a rather hard task at the beginning because she didn't have anything organized, and I needed them organized. After I made a system of where Aunt Sandy was to put her receipts and invoices, it was quick to do the books, and rather easy for me to complete it all in a day, or two. It also gave me extra time to spend with Aunt Sandy, which I loved to do. Besides, I needed that rest and relaxation for my own well-being.

The rest of the time there, I always pitched in helping wherever Aunt Sandy needed help. I always had the feeling of belonging there, and missed it immensely when I had to return to New York City, where it was all concrete, over populated, louder than what I liked, and a much busier life style. I wondered many times if I was really happy living there, with the fast pace, but after I landed my job, I didn't have time to worry about anything else but work. Work became my friend, and at times, my enemy.

It had been a crazy week at the bank, and I was nonstop working from morning to night. I loved my job, but I was too tired to enjoy the night life the city had to offer. I needed a break to collect my thoughts at times, and to figure out what was going on between Phillip and me. I was honestly too tired to even think about that as well.

I had more than a boyfriend/fiance with Phillip. Our

relationship was a very good one at the beginning. Nothing seemed wrong then, he'd ask me to do something with the charm he utilized, and I would do it all, no matter how long it took me to do.

I was now engaged to the most powerful eligible man ever, but there was something not quite right between us lately. I couldn't place my finger on why, or what it was, but it was driving me crazy not knowing what it could be, or if there was anything really wrong at all. I was always aware of my feelings, but this wasn't adding up for some reason. Maybe my mind was getting the best of me, I just didn't know.

Phillip was perfect in every way to me most of the time, but he could also be down right deceitful, extremely rude to his clients, and towards his other employees when he felt like it, and lashed out at me several times that wasn't necessary. It wasn't right what he has been doing to the clients accounts either, which I happened to notice one afternoon. I never have seen Phillip so enraged when I brought it to his attention, telling me if I wanted to get anywhere in life, and especially with him, I needed to keep my mouth shut about what I had seen.

I had asked him about the extra unnecessary, larger than normal, charges on client's statements when I found them, thinking it had to have been a mistake that we could correct easily enough. The glare from Phillip's eyes towards me were piercing enough for me to know, I had opened my mouth when I shouldn't have, and was about to receive a tongue lashing for bringing it to his attention. I was shocked by the way he snapped at me, and I was almost scared enough to consider leaving my job there. I kept my mouth shut from then on, but my eyes and ears were wide open to everything happening around me after that. I started keeping track of the mismanaging amounts I had seen reoccurring over and over by him every month, on my private laptop. I downloaded information, and kept documentation on everything I knew, or heard. Even though I felt guilty about it, I was covering my own butt, and I was beginning to think it was important that I do just that. That was one of the many things I had learned in my college classes, along with all the ramifications that could fall on my shoulders just for knowing illegal activities were happening.

Phillip praised me often by giving me lavish gifts. At first it seemed wonderful, and I gladly accepted each and every one of the gifts, which was mostly jewelry of some sort. I was always seen on his arm when we attended the many benefits and dinner parties, wearing gorgeous outfits fit for a queen with jewelry to match. I had it all, but yet there was that nagging feeling in the pit of my stomach that something wasn't right. I felt it from the moment he chewed me out on the overcharges, that day.

Maybe after my interview it would have been better if I had not accepted the job, and run from him as quick as possible, but there was something about him that was intriguing, and his charm was something else. He knew he had it, and how to use it, that was for sure, and I fell for it like most young single women would, hook, line, and sinker.

I spent most of my nights with him in his penthouse apartment, not far from his bank, after we became engaged. Phillip was CEO and owner of a private banking establishment. He was very well liked, especially by the women, and he knew this tactic, and charmed them with

7

his words to get what he wanted from them. I could see why, as I was the same way when I was hired. The more he smiled talking to me in his deep sexy voice, the more I wanted to do for him. He was handsome, with his dark hair that was beginning to show some gray highlights on his sideburns, and with charisma that oozed with soft spoken words showing as his pearly white teeth glistening when he smiled. The harder I worked, the more money I made, but it was really beginning to zap the life right out of me.

Phillip would have to be away almost weekly on business trips. Those nights I usually spent at my little apartment a few blocks over from the bank in the opposite direction from Phillip's place. I never had any doubt he was getting another high dollar account because that was his goal, to have the best clients known to mankind, and be a multimillionaire in record time. He was on his way to making that happen. No matter what it would take, and being well-known to everyone in the New York area, he was determined on getting his way.

The presentations that I had been assigned to do by him, took long tedious hours of research, in order for him to present to a new client. I would always hope to come along on one of his trips to observe Phillip as he presented the offer, but that never happened. Phillip needed to win the other people over, and that was a "man's place in this dog eat dog world we live in" as he would always tell me.

After about a year of dating Phillip exclusively, he proposed to me at a party he was hosting for the bank employees, after securing the largest account ever. (It was a combination victory party for him with Christmas tied into it, just so he could save a buck.) Never did he recognize who did the work on the projects, and he never intended to give any credit to anyone. He lead everyone to believe he had done the work himself. I tried not to let my feelings show, but I was hurting deeply as I smiled, a fake smile at that. I also knew better than to speak up to claim the work I had done on the projects knowing the repercussions Phillip could inflict on me at a later time.

My engagement ring was amazingly beautiful that he gave me, and the sparkle from it was bright enough to light up a darken room. Oh, I had it made alright. I was on cloud nine dreaming of the day I would become his bride, his wife, but thought after thought of not giving me credit for the work wore heavily on my mind. I felt I deserved recognition of some sort for the long hours I put into each presentation for it to be successfully presented. I never did receive any credit openly, only in the private sector of our lives.

Once everyone came up to congratulate us on our engagement, I put that need to be recognized for the work, out of my mind. I had happier things to think about now, and wasn't going to be consumed of the need for recognition any longer.

For me to be a mother was important too, even though whenever I brought it up to Phillip, he became very distant, and didn't want to talk about having a family. I overheard him talking several times that would never become a father, if he had his way. He wasn't going to be tied down to that kind of responsibility by any means. Now I know how my mother must have felt when my father had left her all alone, pregnant for me. I was hurt by his statements, but then I thought, and hoped maybe, it was him trying to act all macho around his friends.

Joann Buie

$\mathcal{A}$UGUST

New York City was exciting, but the glamour it held was wearing off when I couldn't enjoy the sites, or the many other things I would like to do. I put 125% of my time in working on one presentation report after another for Phillip. I was lucky to get in a Broadway play or the opera once a year, with Phillip complaining all through the performances. Most of the time Phillip reminded me being successful required work, work, work. People need to enjoy their life, and I was finding out how complicated city life was. I wasn't sure I was cut out for that anymore. I was homesick often, which I am sure was because I felt overworked.

I couldn't wait to see Aunt Sandy to show her my beautiful engagement ring, and for her to finally meet the man of my life. Aunt Sandy and I had talked several times during the week, as we always have, but until she met him, it wasn't the same. I told her all the wonderful things about Phillip, but not the things that were nagging me on his work ethics, or his attitude towards people at times. She couldn't wait to meet him in person, and get a chance to see for herself what I have talked to her about on the phone. She seemed pleased for me, which meant a lot. I think I just needed her reassurance that I was making the right decision.

Phillip went with me this last time to visit my aunt and friends, but he snubbed his nose immediately at the place when we pulled in the driveway. He was not very nice to my aunt or friends, as if he thought he was so above them. He made crude remarks and grunted many times in displeasure at just about everything. I told him to quit acting like a baby and to be nice, but that was ignored completely. Needless to say, it didn't go well, and I heard about it for weeks to come from Phillip, when we got back home to New York. He was shocked that I would spend my time there wasting away, when I could be enjoying my life at a real resort overseas. As if I ever had the chance to go anyhow is what I thought. I was so hurt over his actions, and verbal abuse he inflicted on everyone, especially me.

Aunt Sandy never said a bad thing about him to me. I made plenty of excuses and apologies for his rude behavior to everyone all the time, but I think they knew without me uttering another word. I could sense the ill feelings they had when they were around Phillip. I was torn at what to do. Phillip decided to cut our trip down to just the weekend and we headed back to New York City where I spent the rest of my time off, working on yet another presentation report, while Phillip had lunches out with his friends and clients, and many late night meetings throughout the week.

Aunt Sandy was sad and I'm sure very hurt, but said she understood the predicament I was faced with. I was close to tears by the time we said our good-byes. I was resentful towards Phillip for his behavior, but I didn't complain, especially to Phillip over his decision that we had to leave. I knew better than that.

He was trying to get another high dollar client lined up with the bank, and I was working my butt off with the presentation. Phillip had left on another venture to drum up more business again. I was beginning to feel like his personal slave with the presentation report prep work he had me doing so he could just waltz in, get the report to woo over the client as if he worked long and hard on it himself. It was wearing thin on me and yet, I stuck with him for one lame reason or another.

I was happy for his success, but I would have loved to have gone with him now and then to just watch him work. All the work I was doing didn't mean I had to do it at my desk at the bank, but he thought it was best for me to be there. He wanted me to keep an eye on the bank, and on his employees while he was gone. That wasn't necessary because everyone worked hard for him, but yet there was a sense of ease when he was gone. That should have told me something there about how they felt towards Phillip, but I had overlooked everything as if I was totally blind. How could I have been so unseeing about everything? Were we just his puppets on a string, killing ourselves so he could be rich and famous? Everyone was more relaxed with him out of the bank. I was first into work each day, working until late into the night getting everything in order for him.

My best friend and co-worker, Elizabeth, would often

tell me to slow down, and try to get me away from there for lunch, but I usually had her just bring me back a sandwich and iced tea when she came back from her lunch, that allowed me to eat while working at my desk. Elizabeth was such a dear friend to me, and could never understand why I felt I had to stay at the bank. At least once a week during Phillip's absence we would leave work early and take in a movie, and have dinner out. It always felt so good to relax with Elizabeth. No one was the wiser to our friendship, because I always went back to the bank to continue working on the current presentation until around midnight, and I also knew Phillip wouldn't approve of my friendship with anyone from the bank.

Elizabeth and I were very close friends keeping our friendship as quiet as possible. She didn't want the stigma of working her way up the corporate ladder because she was best friends with the owner's fiance. She wasn't like that at all, and I knew I could trust her with things I told her. I never brought up the friendship I had with her to Phillip either, because it went against his beliefs that everyone below his level were just workers, and we didn't have time for workers in our lives. There was a line we weren't to cross, but yet I was friends with Elizabeth none-the-less. I needed a friend many times that could be unbiased of my feelings.

Phillip never called to see how things were going with me, the office, or the current project I was working on the entire time he was gone. When I asked him why he never called while away on any of these trips, he said he was too busy and tired. Once he got back to his room he fell asleep as soon as his head hit the pillow. Besides, he knew I had everything under control. Yep, good ole Lexi could be counted on for everything, every time. I could actually hear him crack that imaginary whip he used to keep us all under control.

Well, that was changed one day, much to my surprise. Phillip couldn't be reached by phone, and not answering his text messages I had sent. The new clients came in a day earlier than scheduled, wanting a preview on what we had done so far, so they could decide if it was worth anymore of their time and money, to work with us or not. I had everything ready for the presentation, but it was for Phillip to pitch the sales with them, not me. However, the client vehemently insisted, so I stepped up to do it myself. After all, it was only a preview, not the whole rock solid presentation which I was sure Phillip would have done, if he could only have been located. I told Elizabeth to set the conference room up, making sure there was a fresh pot of coffee made, and plenty of finger foods available for the clients. I would be back shortly, and if Phillip returned, he could step right in with the information they were seeking.

The presentation was at Phillip's penthouse on the desk where I left it earlier this week so Phillip could glance through it when he got home from his latest business trip. I needed to run there, and retrieve it as fast as I could. It wouldn't take me no more than forty minutes or so, to get it and be back in plenty of time before the clients arrived.

I tried one more time calling Phillip, and it still was going to his voice mail. Leaving him messages that he was ignoring, for some reason, wasn't normally like him. The texts were sent every few minutes with the urgency to respond as soon as possible. Still, nothing. Where could he be, and what could he be doing that was more important than a client's request? I didn't have spare time to worry any longer.

Nothing was making sense, but I knew Phillip wouldn't want to miss selling the clients on this project. It was a huge project that Phillip was sure to make lots of money. Phillip and his money were the most important thing to him.

DECEPTION

I took off immediately from the bank on foot, to Phillip's penthouse to get the report. I was glad the sidewalks weren't full of people making their way to some place themselves that I would bump into. I was in a hurry, it was already humid outside, and I didn't need to be bogged down with people in my way. I rushed inside the building taking the first elevator available to the top floor. Even the elevator seemed to realize I was in a hurry, taking me to the top in no time. Once the elevator doors closed behind me, I dashed to Phillip's office where I left the papers. Grabbing them, and as I turned to leave, I realized I could hear people talking in the other room. Thinking Phillip was home, and probably on his phone, I rushed to our bedroom to get him, so he could do the presentation himself. I stopped dead in my tracks at the doorway, shocked at what was going on in there. Phillip was in our bed with Heather Jenkins, from our bank, making love like two wild animals in heat. They didn't hear me, or see me come in, but their moaning and groaning were horrifying, and hurtful beyond belief.

I knew then what had been nagging at my feelings all this time, and knew I couldn't trust Phillip any longer, knowing I would be calling our engagement off. I lost all respect for him right then and there.

With my heart beating wickedly hard, as if it would burst at any moment, I gathered enough courage, cleared my throat loudly the second as he was nearing his peak of performance pleasure, telling them, "don't stop on my account", as I walked over to the closet jerking my large suitcase out of it. I started throwing my clothes into it haphazardly without even removing them off the hangers. I didn't care how they landed either, knowing they would be full of wrinkles by the time I would be taking them out. I couldn't rush any faster than what I was. The look on their faces were absolutely priceless as they froze when they saw me. I was sure my face was a deep red from the anger that was boiling inside me, but definitely not from embarrassment. I wanted to scream at them, but there wasn't one I could muster up at that time.

They stopped abruptly sitting up trying their best to cover their nakedness, and the shock of someone being in the same room watching what they were doing. I glared at them both telling Phillip I would be out in a few minutes, and they could continue with their heavy panting with moans, and groans, loud enough to wake the dead.

I was amazed how calm I sounded when speaking to them when I was furious on the inside wanting to scream, yell, or even curse at them, but I couldn't get anything out of my mouth for some reason. I knew I needed to stay focused on what was happening, and get everything that belonged to me in my suitcase as quickly as I could, so I could get out of there. The sooner the better.

Phillip was instantly raging mad, shouting at me with everything he could think of, and dear Heather just sat there with a sneering smile across her face that I would have loved to smack off, sending it into the next day. It was apparent that they had been there for most of the week from the amount of room service dishes scattered all over. Some business trip he was attending.

Once I had all my belongings I could find in my suitcase, I headed toward the elevator. Phillip shouted that my last paycheck would be waiting for me to pick up tonight before I left the office, and to be sure I had all my belongings cleaned out of my office as well. He didn't want anything to remind him of me. I figured he'd fire me, but I didn't think he'd do it like this, in front of anyone, but he had, and I had to deal with it for now. Some work ethics he lacked. I saw what was more important to him now. It wasn't me, and he was letting things slide at the bank, which really didn't surprise me when I thought it through. He had me keeping watch on everything at the bank when he was gone, so he didn't miss anything, and I wouldn't even think about going to his place for any reason.

That did it for me though. I closed my eyes standing there like a cold marble statue waiting for the next comment or insult to spew out of his mouth, and they came, one right after another. I knew then there was no way to fix this relationship. It was broken beyond repair, and I was done with him. DONE!! I didn't say anything as he ranted on and on. My throat was painfully dry, as if I had been in the desert on a windy day, making it hard to speak. When he was finally done, I heard Heather giggle, and I walked out never bothering to shut the door behind me.

Once I got inside the elevator with the doors closed, I broke into sobbing tears from the hurt, and I was having difficulty breathing. How could Phillip do something this low to me? I did everything asked of me, and to have this going on behind my back was something I couldn't deal with right then. I made it out the main door of the building still upset, knowing I had to hurry back to the bank, dragging my suitcase behind me. It was as if it was the walk of shame for me at the moment, and I felt everyone was looking at me. There wasn't any time to drop my suitcase off at my apartment, and make it back in time for the meeting, so I had no other choice, but take it with me to my office. That was when it dawned on me, I didn't have to worry anymore about that meeting, I had been fired! It was in Phillip's hands now, and he could deal with it whenever he got to the bank.

The look on my face concerned everyone when I walked into the bank. I must have been a sight to see, but I didn't care. I went straight to my office slamming my door shut as hard as I could. It shattered the window into millions of tiny pieces of glass exploding in the air, and onto the floor. Everyone around the area heard it, and came running over to see what had happened. They said it sounded like something had exploded! I didn't care, not one bit. I was on a mission by then to get out of that bank as fast as I could, with everything I could.

Elizabeth ran into my office immediately to see what was going on, and I broke down crying again, as I told her what I had just walked into at the penthouse. She was shocked, and held me as I cried onto her shoulder. I broke away from Elizabeth, and blew my nose into a tissue, telling what I needed her to get for me. Several new flash drives from the supply room and a box was all I really needed, and to keep an eye open for either Phillip or Heather. I didn't want a nasty scene made at the bank from Phillip. My goal was to get out of there before either one of them returned to the bank.

Elizabeth sent for a box for me to pack my stuff in, but I just opened my suitcase throwing as much as I could into it before the box ever made it up to my office. I wasn't going to wait any longer than necessary to get out of there. I pulled all my information off the computer, all my files, and my notes, and downloaded onto those flash drives. I wiped the history off my computer before popping the flash drives into my purse.

By the time I was about to walk out of my office, Mary from payroll, was there with my final paycheck. She had been crying as well, and hugged me telling me how sorry she was that it came to this, and they were all going to miss me tremendously. I don't know what reason Phillip gave her, but she probably could read between the lines easily. Mary told me she counted all my overtime, vacation days, sick days never taken, and my severance pay, according to the outline in Phillip's employee handbook, which put me over to where I was fully vested into the company. She winked at me as I took the check. I went straight to the teller cashing it. I didn't even look to see how much it was, and at that point I really didn't care. It would show on my receipt, and that was all I needed for now. I withdrew everything I had, closing both my savings and checking accounts as well, and said my goodbyes to everyone I could.

I didn't hold back the reason I was leaving. Several had asked, and I told them why, and who I caught Phillip in bed with. Probably not the most dignified way for me to say anything about it, but I really didn't care. The fact I was fired by Phillip, me not being a quitter, made me feel better if they knew what a conniving jerk Phillip is, and a sleaze Heather turned out to be. It may have made me look like a fool, or a scorned person right then, but I didn't care, not anymore.

Elizabeth summoned a cab for me, and as soon as it arrived, I was gone from there. Gone for good. I will never step into that building ever again. I took one last look at the bank just as my cab pulled away from the curb. It hurt to leave there, but it was now in my past.

I arrived at my own apartment in a matter of minutes, and the doorman helped me out of the cab retrieving my suitcase at the curb, and the bellboy carried it up to my apartment. I quickly pulled my drapes closed tight, and bolted my door shut. Phillip had a key so I needed to make plans immediately. Not sure if he would have the boldness to show up, but I didn't want to take any chances either. I didn't want to ever see him again. EVER!!

Slowly I gained control of my shattered life, emotions, and thought things through a little more clearer, as Elizabeth had suggested I do, when I was getting into the cab. I was crushed, hurt, betrayed, and downright humiliated beyond what I could express. I never felt so lonely as I did right then, and I had no one I could turn to right now. I needed to think, and get what I needed done immediately, so I could get out of New York.

Once I was over my self pity party, I needed to take charge

of my life for the first time since coming to New York. I hadn't realized how Phillip had control over everything I had done since he hired me. I was nothing but a puppet on strings for him to manipulate as he wanted. Well, those strings have been cut now, and I'm free to be myself once again.

Safety First

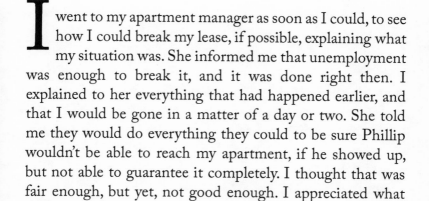

I went to my apartment manager as soon as I could, to see how I could break my lease, if possible, explaining what my situation was. She informed me that unemployment was enough to break it, and it was done right then. I explained to her everything that had happened earlier, and that I would be gone in a matter of a day or two. She told me they would do everything they could to be sure Phillip wouldn't be able to reach my apartment, if he showed up, but not able to guarantee it completely. I thought that was fair enough, but yet, not good enough. I appreciated what they could do for me, but I knew I had to get out and away, as soon as possible for my own well being, and especially for my safety.

Before I went back up to my apartment, I stopped to tell Darrell, the doorman, not to allow Phillip upstairs stating that I was fearful for my life from him. I gave Darrell a large tip for all he has done for me throughout the years, and knew I could count on him to follow through with my wishes the best he could.

Elizabeth called right before she left work that night wanting to come over to my apartment to see me. She knew how upset I was when I left the bank, and she was worried as well. She used her own cell phone to make the call so no one could trace her call to me, bringing Chinese take out with her, and a bottle of wine to help with the heartache I was feeling. I could drown my sorrows with the wine, celebrate my new independence, or both. Which ever I decided would be appropriate while we drank it.

Elizabeth informed me after I had left the bank, Phillip came in tempestuously mad that I was gone, and pretty peeved about glass all over the floor from my shattered door window that maintenance was busy vacuuming up. It was only a matter of time before that window would give out. I had placed several repair orders to maintenance over the years, and it had been over looked all this time. Something would have to be done with it now, because there was no way to get around not replacing it. Everyone throughout the bank had already heard by then what had happened to me, and stayed a safe distance all afternoon from both Phillip, and Heather.

Phillip tried to put a block on my accounts once he learned how much Mary wrote the check for, learning I had cashed it already. I had also closed my checking, and savings accounts, at the same time. It was too much money for me to be carrying around, but that was a chance I had to take. I was one step ahead of Phillip when it came to my money. The audacity of him thinking he could place a hold my money, the money I had worked hard for.

The clients came in for their review when they said they would, but Phillip had nothing to show them. Phillip had absolutely no clue why there were there, or what they wanted. He didn't know they were waiting for him the entire time while he was ranting to everyone about me leaving him high and dry. Eventually, they got up walking out in the middle of everything happening in disgust. They had told Phillip they were taking their business elsewhere. It couldn't have happened to a better person. Guess Phillip should have answered his phone, or text messages, instead of turning it off when he did so it wouldn't disturb him, and Heather's activities. Serves him right to be blind-sighted for once in his life.

Heather acted as if nothing was wrong when she came waltzing in, going directly to her office, and immediately closing her door behind her. She must have thought she dodged a bullet, but little did she know that everyone had already heard what had happened. Elizabeth said Heather acted so surprise to learn I wasn't there any longer. Elizabeth thought she could have won an Oscar award for the acting she did in front of everyone already. Elizabeth made no bones about telling her I had been fired, and most people at the bank knew why too. Heather jerked her head toward Elizabeth, with the look of hate seething in her eyes, as she screamed at her to get out of her office. Elizabeth smiled at Heather, and gladly did exactly as she had been told, smiling ear to ear as she walked out.

After Elizabeth left my apartment that night to go home, I stayed up making my plans. I had no other place to go, but home. Phillip knew this too, and I was sure he was probably laughing to himself over my dilemma. He could laugh all he wanted because I would be fine being home, and there was nothing he could do about that. He lost his control over me, and would never get a chance at having it back.

I rushed down to the electronic store not far from my apartment that was open 24 hours a day, and bought myself two burner phones. It was only a matter of time Phillip would realize, if he hadn't already, that I took his cell phone with me when I packed my belongings at his penthouse. I did it intentionally because I wanted to see what he had been texting, especially to Heather, and mostly when their relationship had started. I knew Phillip would be having the phones shut off once he realized that I probably took his with me. I couldn't wait to have his SIM card removed placing it into the burner phone. Before I left the store, it was all done for me, before he could do anything about it. He had a new SIM card in his phone with nothing on it, nothing!! I didn't want to take any chances. I bought the other burner phone for my own personal calls, so he couldn't trace me in any possible way to my location. I understood technology more than what he ever gave me credit for, that was for sure.

I grabbed several items I needed immediately from the store like shampoo, tooth brush, tooth paste, a hair brush, some Pepsi, and bubble bath crystals, before going back to my apartment. That was when my land line phone started to ring non-stop. Wonder how long that had been happening, and just as I expected, it was Phillip. I let it go to voice mail deciding I would listen to it later, maybe. When I did finally listen to all the messages he left, he was in explosive rage with his words, and hateful accusations. His biggest concern was how I had embarrassed him in front of Heather, and the clients he lost. I scuffed at that message that I had embarrassed him, well, I think the shoe was on the other foot...mine! I knew I was in for trouble with him. I felt unsafe, and knew the sooner I was away, the better and safer I would feel.

I was really getting scared, because of what his threats were. He didn't consider them threats, just promises he planned to fulfill in his calls. I quickly finished packing my belongings in my suitcases. I had a furnished apartment, so I didn't have to worry about the furniture, just my own personal belongings.

Once I finished packing all my possessions, I had the front desk call a taxi to take me to the airport. I wasn't really going to go to the airport to leave, but I wasn't going to leave any trail for Phillip to find me. Phillip was very powerful, and down right ugly now. I couldn't take a chance with him any longer.

As soon as I said my goodbyes to the few people on duty at my apartment building, I got in the cab telling the driver to drive to the airport. Several feet down the street I turned around in the seat, and saw Phillip hop out of his limo to my apartment building. I couldn't have planned my departure any sooner, or any better.

The cab driver helped remove my luggage at the airport curb, and I made my way inside as he drove away. I waited about ten minutes before hailing another cab outside the airport terminal, to take me to the Holiday Inn, by the airport where I got a room under my grandmother's maiden name. I planned to stay there for a few days to get some much needed sleep, and where I could I plan out the rest of my leaving New York. Everything was happening too fast for me to plan everything out at once. My brain was in overload at the moment, and it needed to slow down to do things correctly. I knew I was going back home, there was no question about that, but I needed to keep my plans to myself. I needed to do it my way, just to be safe.

I slept until after one o'clock the next afternoon waking up hungry and clear headed, which I needed to be until I departed from New York. I ordered room service for my meals keeping on the safe side, and watched a movie on the TV while I ate. I was relaxing for the first time in years, and I was going to enjoy it as much as possible, while I could.

My time would be limited there, as I knew Phillip pretty good, and knew what he was capable of doing to seek my location. I knew he couldn't track me with the phones, because I cured that problem last night.

After I took a long hot bubble bath, I decided it would be best if I left sometime the next day or two. I didn't want to delay it any longer than necessary.

I had the desk call a cab for me the following day, and went back to the airport where I rented a car. From there I drove to a dealership to purchase a vehicle for myself. I found the SUV I wanted. I made the best deal I could make, and paid cash for it. The dealership wasn't happy about the cash because they make more money from financing it. I also declined all the additional things they tried to sell me to increase the cost. I didn't want the extended warranties. I also didn't want the warranties they offered for tire and wheel damage, or the dentless paint repair package. I know they make a ton of money on those items. I didn't fall for it. The factory warranty would just have to do for now. With all my paperwork done, and my new car ready to be handed over to me, I phoned the rental car company to come pick up the rental car at the dealership, and I drove back to the Holiday Inn in my brand new vehicle. Now all that was left before leaving in the morning was a good nights sleep.

This was draining for me, and I was eager for sleep. As I laid there, I got to thinking of my new vehicle getting broken into, damaged, or stolen from the parking lot. This was a new worry for me because I never had a new car before. Come to think about it, I never even owned a vehicle before, and the way my luck has been running at the moment, I was expecting the worse to happen.

I finally fell asleep sometime later, probably from being fully exhausted.

LEAVING NEW YORK BEHIND

———❦•• ◆ ••❧———

Early the next morning I had breakfast in my room while I finished packing the last of my stuff, soon I was on my way home to Michigan, and to Aunt Sandy. The sky was gray and wet, an exact match on how I was feeling at the moment. Even though I had slept through the night, it wasn't a restful sleep. So many thoughts raced through my head about Phillip, myself, leaving New York, and the drive ahead of me. I had so many things to think about that were weighing heavy on my mind at the moment, but decided the sooner out of here, the better.

I wasn't sure if leaving was the right thing for me to do now. Maybe I should go back to the bank, and confront Phillip with everything, and get it all out of my system. Deep down in my heart I knew that could be dangerous for me, and it would only add fuel to the fire for Phillip. I hate having second thoughts on any situation. Aunt Sandy thought the best thing for me to do was just to get out of there, so I'm taking her advise, leaving while I can.

I called Aunt Sandy on my burner phone the first night this all began, because the company phone had been turned off. I expected it would be, once Phillip realized I had his phone. That was how Phillip worked. If things didn't go his way, he did everything in his power to take control of people. He would try to discredit them in any way he could. He was like a playground bully getting what he wanted, no matter who it hurt, even close friendships were not off limits. He believed in a scorched earth policy with absolutely no remorse. Thinking of how he was, I cannot believe I did not see this before. Maybe I did, but just didn't want to believe it.

I suppose it was eating at him that he couldn't find me right now. That was a good feeling thinking about that, and I actually had a grin on my face when I thought about it. I decided to keep that in my mind while I drove away. Made it easier for me to leave everything behind that I worked so hard to get. Some might think I was a coward for doing it this way, but I know in my heart, it was the best way for me. I didn't feel as if I was running away from anything, but I did feel like I was running for my well being.

I mailed Phillip's phone back to him, from the airport the day before, along with my company phone, which I had removed all information from, and took the SIM card out. I didn't bother to insure them, or the package. I simply put them in a padded envelope figuring if they broke, oh well, they broke. Too bad!! What's a broken phone compared to a broken heart.

I filled Aunt Sandy in on a few things the first night after I got my new phone. Also told her under no circumstances, what so ever, was she to tell Phillip anything about my plans or where I was holed up. Not my new cell phone number, not to mention I had even called her, not that I was coming home, how I was getting home, nothing, nothing, NOTHING!!! He didn't need to know anything about me any longer. I was in control of my life now, not him, and besides, he blew it with me by cheating with Heather.

Aunt Sandy didn't question me very much as she listened, and fully understood how important it was that Phillip not know anything about me, or my location. I know she had to be relieved that I'm no longer engaged to that jerk, but she would never say so. At least not right now. I could tell by the tone of her voice, that she was happy for me on that aspect, but concerned for me, and angry as well, when I told her what had happened after catching Phillip and Heather in our bed together. I will have plenty of time to tell her every graphic detail once I get home.

I'm figuring it will take me at least two solid days driving to get there, as I don't plan to rush the drive. All my possessions, and all my information from my office desk, were neatly tucked away in the back of my SUV, still giving me ample room to lay down if I got tired. I didn't want to take a chance of my vehicle getting broken into by leaving anything in my car to get a motel room, and I didn't want to haul everything into a room for the night either. I was so paranoid now that Phillip would find me, and I was determined that wasn't going to happen.

During the time I was driving home, my mind was thinking about everything that had happened. It hit me then why Phillip was so adamant about not being friends with the other people in the bank, but he did with me, and also with

Heather. He had double standards when it involved him. It reminded me of that phrase, "Do as I say, not as I do". Why I didn't think about that until now made me wonder how many other things had I been blind about. If I thought hard about it, I could probably come up with a million things I over-looked while working there.

I also thought of revenge, and all the things I knew that would get him into deep trouble with his bank accounting practices. I wanted to hurt him, as he has hurt me, but on a higher level. Hurt him in areas he never thought possible, mainly in the wallet. I lost all my love for him immediately that day when I saw him with Heather in our bed. I don't understand how he could do this to me. Apparently, I hadn't meant anything to him.

Aunt Sandy said I needed to get that nonsense out of my head. In due time something would happen where he would regret everything, and everyone he had done wrong in the past. I could only hope.

I couldn't believe how many things I over looked for Phillip. I hadn't told anyone the many things he had done with several funds he had, the client's bills he over charged and the high risk investment trades he made without the client's knowledge. He got away with so much, and yet he always came out of everything smelling like a rose, and climbed higher in the banking field. I swear, he will get caught sometime. I just have to be patient for that time, and it will happen, that I was sure of.

The first night I slept was in a rest area somewhere in northeast Ohio. It wasn't too bad, but I was awaken with every noise possible, so I really didn't get the rest I needed. Small meals, snack foods, and several cups of hot black coffee were all drive-through windows orders, and gas to fill up was quickly done. I'd run into the restroom only when needed, and was out in less than five minutes tops. I felt semi-confident my stuff would still be in my vehicle when I got back in, although I took my laptop, and my purse with the flash drives in it, everywhere with me regardless.

I drove the rest of the way home that day, and as exhausted as I was, I made it there without any problems. As I pulled in the driveway, I could see Aunt Sandy was busy working under the covered pavilion on what looked like shutters off the house. She smiled broadly and waved, as she directed me straight into the garage so I wouldn't have to unpack anything right away. The only thing I remember saying to her was, "sleep now, talk later", and went straight to my bedroom falling fast asleep on my own bed. I slept good knowing I was away from Phillip, and in the safety of my own room. Safe with the people around me that genuinely loved me.

I woke up to Maria, Aunt Sandy's hired helper with the house and cabins, clanging things around in the kitchen making dinner, and the aroma was absolutely fabulous that filtered up to my room. Aunt Sandy was glad to see me awake and ready to eat, hoping I had a good appetite when I came down from my bedroom. That, I assured them, I did have. As the three of us sat down to the table, I noticed the table was set for four. No sooner I thought that, the door opened with Tommy walking in to join us.

All I could do was stare at him as he washed up and took his seat. I had no idea he was still around here helping Aunt Sandy. He smiled saying hello to each of us as he sat down telling Maria everything smelled delicious. I had to remember my manners by closing my mouth enough to hear Aunt Sandy say grace, and to quit staring at him.

Aunt Sandy had hired an older gentleman to help her long ago named Thomas Michael. I was a young teenager at the time. She hired Mr. Michael to help around the resort with anything and everything she couldn't do herself. He was a very nice older man with the bluest eyes that seemed to twinkled all the time, with such a kind friendly smile, and disposition to match. His hair was snow white that made his tanned arms really stand out. He had lost his wife many years prior, and was needing a simple job he would enjoy, that he could do easily. The job at the resort fit the bill for both him, and my aunt.

Thomas Michael also had custody of his grandson, Tommy, through an ugly custody battle with his parents, which he won. Once Child Protection Service had found Tommy alone in the house during the winter with no heat in the house, no food to eat, and no way for Tommy to get help if he needed, they stepped in contacting Mr. Michael making him aware of the situation. Tommy's parents were at the bar drunk or high on drugs, so Mr. Michael stepped in taking Tommy away from that. They both lived in a smaller cabin at Aunt Sandy's resort, close to the house working for rent and meals. I knew Aunt Sandy had him on payroll since I had done the books, and noticed it wasn't a large amount of earnings Mr. Michael received. That was because the cabin, and meals, were a part of his payment. Just enough extra spending money for him to enjoy life, and to buy his night crawler worms he needed for fishing on his time off.

Tommy and I were pretty close to the same age, and at one time we were known to be a couple of crazy love struck teenagers. I thought Tommy was so cute back then, always happy when he was around, and we had a great time together. He was my everything at that time, until I went away to college and stayed in New York City after graduation. I think Aunt Sandy was relieved I went to college out of state, and I had stayed away for a few reasons. I often wonder if that was why she pushed me to attend college there? One reason was of how serious Tommy and I were about each other and after catching us in bed one time, she knew of the possible ramifications it could have had on my future, if I hadn't left when I did.

I had never been so embarrassed as I was that day getting caught, but Aunt Sandy just told me to get dressed and finish my chores, as she closed the door behind her. I was so worried I would be sent away after that, but Aunt Sandy decided it was better that we talk about it openly when she decided it was time to talk. Maybe she had to calm down herself before she spoke to me, I don't know, but it was later that night when we went to the swing on the beach.

Aunt Sandy was very calm when she talked to me, and explained how she felt when walking in on us like she had, but she never yelled at me, like she probably should have. I think it would have been easier on me if she had yelled. Just the thought I had let her down was hard on me mentally. She also understood that it wasn't the first time it had ever happened to anyone my age either. Times have changed since she was my age. At least she was understanding of that, and of my feelings towards Tommy. I never wanted to let her down again, not ever.

Every time I went home on vacation, Tommy was never around. I often wondered if it was Aunt Sandy's way of keeping us apart, and me not getting pregnant at a young age. I was okay with that, even though I didn't understand it at the time. I was mad, and hurt all balled into one. Once I was engaged to Phillip, I didn't think about Tommy as much anymore. Tommy was my first love, and I always felt he would always be special to me, no matter what.

A few years later Aunt Sandy, and Mr. Michael were married. Aunt Sandy had her new husband and Tommy move into the house with her. Tommy took the room next to mine, and we shared a bathroom between the rooms. Aunt Sandy was so happy with everything, and I was happy for her. I called him Uncle Thomas immediately, which he was thrilled I had accepted him in the family, as I gave him the biggest hug ever wishing the best for him and my aunt, when they were married. They were married on the beach at the resort at sunset, just as the sun hit the horizon. It was so beautiful. Maria stood up for her, and Tommy for his grandfather. That was the last time I had seen Tommy, until now, since I had left to go back to New York.

There didn't seem to be anything between Tommy and me anymore, and I didn't press the issue with him, or anyone else. He stayed his distance from me, but I would catch him looking at me whenever I looked his way. I didn't say anything to him either, which I suppose I could have, but I didn't. I wasn't sure if I wanted to know anything about him, or the fact maybe we still had a spark of love between us yet. I dropped that topic immediately because I was never going to love a man again.

Uncle Thomas died a few years later leaving my aunt heartbroken once again. Aunt Sandy explained to me later that night that she asked Tommy to stay on at the resort, and he filled in where Uncle Thomas left off at running the equipment, and doing the various jobs Aunt Sandy couldn't do. She said Tommy never hesitated at that offer and stepped right in where his grandfather left off, at doing the work around the resort.

Aunt Sandy was the only person that he considered family to him, and she felt the same way towards him. However, I would have thought Aunt Sandy would have told me that little detail of him still being at the resort working for her, but she hadn't.

He had gone to college himself years ago and passed the bar exam, but never tried to get into a firm to work for, or take on a job representing anyone on his own. He was content working for Aunt Sandy. I think he was looking after her for his grandfather, as he had promised he would. It was working out for them, but no one told me he was still living there.

I was however, pleasantly surprised and my, how handsome he was now. He matured in more ways than one and grew at least a foot since we saw each other last. No more acne and had muscles that bulged with every movement he made and the tightness in his shirt displayed a very firm abdomen. That scrawny kid of my past, grew into a full grown man. A very nice looking man at that, I thought.

Dinner was rather quiet and after Maria cleared the table, she left to go home to her husband with a plate of food for him. Aunt Sandy and I were finally able to talk about what had happened in New York alone. As we took our glasses of iced tea, we walked towards the beach settling in on the porch swing there. We were able to talk openly as most of her guests were still having their meals themselves leaving the beach rather deserted of people.

Just hearing the waves lap the shore line was usually soothing to me, yet it didn't feel like it tonight as I spilled everything out between the tears that flowed, to Aunt Sandy. I was so glad she sat with me and just listened, shaking her head in disbelief. I didn't need anything else, other than to get it all out of me. She was so kind not to be judgmental as she listened carefully to everything I said.

When I thought I was done talking, I thought of something else I had to say and cried some more. I don't remember how long we were on the beach, with Aunt Sandy holding my hand listening to me, but she had the entire time.

Aunt Sandy informed me that Phillip had called several times looking for me when I was done telling her everything. She told me she played dumb as to what had happened between the two of us as I had hoped she would. Phillip told her we had nothing than a little misunderstanding, and he wanted to talk to me as soon as he could. At first Aunt Sandy was about to give him a piece of her mind, but knew right away Phillip would have known she had heard from me, and she didn't want him having that information. He also told her that when she did hear from me, to let me know things weren't over between us, and he wanted his things back immediately, or else. Or else what, Aunt Sandy wondered. I didn't have anything that belonged to him. (He broke our engagement as far as I was concerned, and I kept the ring thinking I could pawn it later, or sell it at a jewelry store). All the reports were my work which I merely just kept a file on what I had wrote, for my own personal use. I didn't have any plans to use them myself for anything, but knew it was important for me to have a copy. (Could he be talking about the flash drives? All two of them?) Little did I know then, how smart that was for me to have them. I was very tired that night, and also a big weight had been lifted off my shoulders by talking to Aunt Sandy. Sleep was waiting for my head to hit my pillow, where I didn't think about anything else.

I didn't want Phillip to drag Aunt Sandy into any of his mind controlling games, and expressed that information with her. I didn't want him showing up at the resort either. This was the end of the busy time there for Aunt Sandy and she had plenty on her plate already. Especially with me and my extra baggage showing up like I had.

*E*MOTIONS

I made several calls to Elizabeth during the week and she filled me in on all the news and gossip, going on at the bank. Several people had already quit for "better opportunities", as they didn't think much of Phillip anymore. I think everyone knew how shrewd he could be, and didn't want to be his puppet any longer themselves. They were smart! Elizabeth said the people had felt if Phillip could do what he did to me, they realized what he could do to them, if he wanted. They didn't want to take a chance of losing their job that way, so they left on their own accord, and they all had other jobs lined up in advance.

Heather had moved into my office immediately, and was constantly gone from her desk instead of doing her job. She was always giving Elizabeth the work that she didn't want to do, or just couldn't do herself. Elizabeth was also searching for employment elsewhere, and as soon as she obtains one, she'll be gone too. That was between the two of us, because she planned to leave without Phillip catching wind of it ahead of time. Since Elizabeth and I kept our friendship quiet, she felt pretty safe, so far, from anything bad happening to her. What made it nice was that Elizabeth heard all the things from everyone without them knowing it would definitely get back to me.

The profit margin had also dropped at the bank since I left. I wish I could take credit for that, but I knew in reality I had nothing to do with it. Apparently, Phillip had lost a few large accounts by this whole ordeal, and was gone so much trying to either retrieve the accounts, or looking for new clients to replace the ones he lost. Phillip's presentation reports weren't as precise as mine, so they didn't show as the ones I researched and wrote, according to Elizabeth anyway. Elizabeth knew it was Heather who was doing the presentation reports for him, after she had Elizabeth get the information requested, but it was pretty obvious they weren't as precise as mine had been. Heather would have a hard time finding her way out of a paper bag if she had to! Karma is such a wonderful bliss!!

Phillip was trying to make me pay for the broken glass from my office window. Elizabeth reminded him I had placed several requests in to maintenance to have it repaired, but no one came to do it. Talk was spreading fast he was going to take me to small claims court for it, but that rumor had been squashed when maintenance informed him I had a solid alibi on having it repaired, with Phillip telling them himself it wasn't necessary, and to hold off on it. Once Phillip read where I had placed several work orders to have the window repaired, not allowing him to have a leg to stand on. I don't think he thought about that, and finally quit pursuing the claim any longer. I also kept the copies of the work orders for some reason. Good thing!!

I kept so much information on the work, billings, ethics, or lack of, and on the projects I did myself, so if Phillip wants a problem, let him bring it on, I'm ready for it. One of the first things I learned in my business classes was to... document, document, document to cover thy own ass, and find a way to take ownership of the work. My professor said several times to drill it into our heads, if we were going to take the time to do the work, take the time to be proud of it, and own it.

I also know that Phillip had been seeing Heather shortly after Phillip and I had become engaged. No wonder he was never in the "mood" to set a wedding date, he had no intentions of us ever being married. All those times he was away for business, Heather was also gone from her office, and now it didn't take much to know why he never wanted me to go along. What a fool I had been. Phillip had my heart completely, and I trusted him with all his words. Words that were nothing but lies, and full of deceit!! I will never make that mistake again either! NEVER!!! Phillip had used me for his gain, and I was so stupid to not see it as it happened over and over and over.

Now I was able to realize why my mom could never trust a man again, by what has happened to me in my own situation. Even though it wasn't over a pregnancy like hers had been, it was over the deceit from a man. Love does strange things to your mind, and if the guy couldn't be honest himself, it wasn't worth it. I think my mom would have gone after Phillip with her finger nails extended, if she was still alive, too. I don't know what she would have done to him, but I know it wouldn't have been pretty.

My mom made it through life the best she could at raising me being a single parent, and I know deep in my heart, I will be able to go on myself in time. Once I get over the hurt I feel, I can, and will be better. We were strong women, and nothing could stop us from what we wanted in life. I know my mom didn't want to die when she did, but she held on as long as she could. Her love, courage, and determination, was undeniably the things I admired most about her. I was only eight years old when she passed, but I understood what she had told me more than what most eight year old kids probably could have. Maybe it was because I was brought up in an adult world that I understood, but regardless, I sure need her now.

I told Aunt Sandy and Maria, what Elizabeth passed on to me earlier that day. Maria rolled her eyes, and scoffed at it by blowing air out of the tiny slit in her mouth. She made no bones about it, that Phillip made the hair on her arms rise when he was there for that one, and only weekend. She did not like him one iota, and she was beyond thrilled I was no longer with him. She saw him as a sleaze bag out to hurt people, and get what he wants no matter how he gets it, legal or not. She swore his time was limited on what he was doing, and when he falls, he was going to go down hard, and fast. It wasn't going to be a pretty sight either. She ended what she had to say by saying, "just mark my words on that".

I had never known Maria to be so vocal on anything serious before, so this was interesting to hear her spout off on her feelings about Phillip. If other people could see this happening, why couldn't I, I wondered. I refused to think I was that naive about Phillip, but I must have been.

I had to agree with Maria about Phillip getting caught down the line. When it came to his work ethics, he was always looking through rose colored glasses thinking he was the best, knew everything, knew loop holes for everything else, and was untouchable by anyone, including the law. He will be caught being the weasel he is, and I'm glad I won't be around the bank when that happens. That will be an ugly scene for sure.

SEPTEMBER AND OCTOBER

After several days passed, I began helping Aunt Sandy with everything around the resort, and it felt somewhat good. I was beginning to find myself once again, and the happiness the resort always brought to me. I still kept my guard up for Phillip showing up, but it didn't seem likely he was going to. It was an awful feeling to have to keep looking over your shoulder for the possibility of Phillip being there, and what he would do, or say to me. I didn't feel completely comfortable knowing he could, if he wanted to. It wasn't something I looked forward to either, but knew it was only a matter of time when he probably would feel the need to confront me. It was always his way, he needed that.

When I went to town, I would make it look as if I was window shopping when in reality, I was glancing at the reflection the store windows provided, to be sure Phillip wasn't lurking behind me. What a horrible way to feel, but the trust in him was gone and I wouldn't put anything past him to try something to hurt me even more.

Autumn was quickly approaching with temperatures dropping at night, yet comfortable during the daytime. Aunt Sandy was busy with the cabins she would be renting out to the hunters, as they made their way up north from the Detroit area. It was usually the same group of men every year, which were a nice bunch of guys. They were always either hunting or going out to eat, which made it easy for us. They hunted on private land, and it happened to be across the road from us, that they all co-owned, allowing them to be able to hunt whenever. How convenient for them, but how nice for us. The additional income during the off season was a plus in our books.

Aunt Sandy remarked that football season is just around the corner, and reminded me how we loved watching the games together. She had every snack known to mankind to munch on while watching the games, too. Before she married Uncle Thomas, he would always come in to enjoy the games with us and Tommy would tag along. Sometimes Maria would bring her husband Fred, over as well, and it was such a great time.

I was glad they had kept the Sunday afternoon tradition of watching the football games together all these years. It was always loud, and exciting watching the games with them.

I hadn't watched a football game since leaving for New York. Phillip thought it was a complete waste of time stating only morons watched something so lame, as a football game. He probably didn't even understand the game to begin with.

I was usually too busy working on a presentation report for him to even bother turning the TV on to watch, or just listen to the game. Come to think about it, I was working almost every single day of the year missing out on many things I had enjoyed doing before.

It's strange I didn't think much about working everyday until I had left the job. I realized that more often, as time went on, feeling like I had been just a puppet for Phillip. I was his personal slave. He had me doing everything, and I did it just to please him. He was the one who was able to do things whenever he wanted while I was stuck on his projects. He was traveling, eating at fine restaurants all the time, socializing with important people, and all the time I was home by myself, usually eating a peanut butter and jelly fold over so I could work longer on a report for him. So blind I was.

I wasn't sure how I would like watching the football games now though. The team players were all different, but Aunt Sandy was a die hard fan of her Green Bay Packers, win or lose. I asked why she didn't cheer for the Detroit Lions, since we were living in Michigan. Aunt Sandy explained that Uncle Darren was from Wisconsin, and a huge Packer fan right from the start of their relationship. After they got married she started watching the games with him and ever since then, she was a Packer fan. Maybe it was in memory of her late husband, it doesn't matter. She loved the Packers still, and no one was going to persuade her to follow a different team.

We always cheered the Packers on no matter what. Aunt Sandy would get so excited when there was a touchdown, and very sour when the other team would score, shouting at the TV as if someone might hear her and over turn the penalties, or even the score!! She was such a hoot to be around though, and I loved being around her very much.

Aunt Sandy had been busy putting her autumn decorations up outside during the day. She was big on the idea the resort had to be decorated for all the holidays, and had all the decorations stored from year to year in the attic above the garage. She felt it was a reflection on her, and her resort. I hadn't even noticed them already up, until one night when I pulled into the driveway after dark from picking up a few things from the store for myself. Everything looked so nice, and once I stepped out of my car, I could feel the crisp autumn evening air with a hint of a few log burning fireplaces burning.

The air was so different here. It had a natural woodsy scent, where New York was quite stuffy to me. Here we had the open skies, where in the big city, it was just tall buildings from one end to the other. The darken clouds in the sky gave it the eerie feeling of Halloween being right around the corner, and just lights from the street in all different colors in the city. I can't remember ever looking at the sky during the different seasons while in the city. Well, maybe to see if it was going to rain or not, but never paid that much attention to it otherwise.

I hadn't adjusted to being back home completely, and I hadn't gotten out of my self pity mood I was in most of the time either. Maybe I liked being in this mood, I really don't know anymore, but it was a self destructive mood far from what I had been like before Phillip came into my life.

Many days went by in such a blur as if I was just going through the motions of being awake, and I was ready to go to bed as soon as it got dark enough. Sleeping was my only escape from everything that happened, and it brought me comfort knowing I was in my own bed.

I could hear Aunt Sandy and Maria talking in the early mornings with their concern over me. I walked in on them doing so one day, and politely asked them not to talk about me when I was around because it only made me feel worse. I know they were concerned about me, but this was something I had to do on my own, my own way. I don't know what could release me from the hold Phillip still had over me, but I also knew I had to get on with my life, some how.

I spoke less and less to Elizabeth, thinking that was the string that kept me attached to my past five years, and I needed to move on. It wasn't just that or her, it was everything about my last five years that represented what I wished I could have changed. I felt I wasted too much time and energy trying to please everyone else, that I didn't have time to please, or take care of myself.

I never thought of Phillip being in control of everything, but now when I think about everything, I realize he was. I didn't go anywhere he didn't like me to go, dressed the way he wanted me to, and stayed mostly cooped up in the apartment working on the project reports for him. He would be out on the town enjoying himself telling me it was for the business, and I actually believed him. Was I a fool or what? I was completely blind that he was out actually enjoying himself. Why not, he had his personal slave at home working for him, me.

I know he couldn't have been with new clients all those nights either. That wasn't how he worked. Who knows if he wasn't with Heather all those times. I now believe he was with her, and just flat out lied to me. I checked my forehead in the mirror to see if their was a large "L" across it for loser, because that's what I was, and how I was feeling. How could someone who claims to love someone, do the despicable stuff to the one he supposedly wanted to share his life with?

I've had plenty of time to think these past few weeks with everything slowing down, and realizing how I was used and taken advantage of. My ideas were great ideas, and that was all Phillip had me around for. I didn't need him to haunt me any longer. I needed to accept that fact, and get on with making my life better, for me. By my sulking so much, Phillip was still in control of me, and I was still losing the battle. But, it was still nagging at my every thought.

I heard everyone in the living room watching the football game Sunday late morning, and they seemed to be having a great time. I knew without even looking at the TV that the Packers were winning, just from listening to Aunt Sandy squealing with excitement. Everyone was having fun, while I laid on my bed trying to tune out life itself.

I finally got up and went outside, just before halftime to sit on the swing at the beach by the water. It was calm and relaxing there, even though it was very chilly. I was deep in thought thinking I have lost my mind on everything and everyone, and especially on myself. I have been so down for weeks, even thinking maybe I should see a doctor, but that wasn't me either. I didn't need anyone else knowing I'm a loser. I failed a good relationship with Tommy years ago, and I failed being engaged to Phillip. Mostly I feel I failed myself for letting things get so out of hand, and not knowing what to do. I was a lost soul without any goals to continue on.

A few minutes later I heard footsteps approaching, and

it was Aunt Sandy coming to check on me. I rolled my eyes as she made her presence known, as she sat down next to me on the swing. That wasn't like me to do that, not towards my aunt, but I had. She has been nothing but good to me all my life, and she surely didn't deserve that. She had noticed my eye rolls, and asked if she was intruding. I apologized saying she was fine, it was just me having a bad day, and I apologized for the eye rolls.

She sat next to me on the swing chatting about the game, and was wishing I'd join them, but knew that probably wasn't going to happen. Not today for sure. She went back to the house to watch the second half of the game, and said we could talk later if I felt up to it.

Now, I felt like everyone was walking around me on eggshells trying not to hurt my feelings, and give me space. Was I that fragile, ready to go over the deep edge if someone upset me, or came into my space uninvited?

Aunt Sandy said something that made me think long and hard, before she left me on the swing. She had said I was not only hurting myself, but I was hurting those around me that loved me. The ones that truly loved me with all their heart. I was only trying to punish myself for the mishaps in New York. Aunt Sandy said I was not a failure when I told her that, because I gave it my all, was very successful at my job, and a good honest person. I was caught in the web of deceit and lies, from Phillip. Not everyone is like him, and many other people probably saw through his games. Everyone but me, I thought.

It made me think for several days on how right she was. One morning I decided to hell with Phillip, and my time in New York. I could be successful where ever I went, if I wanted, and when I feel like I have the need to do it again, I knew I could. There was nothing that was stopping me, and it didn't have to be in New York. I was not going to let Phillip win at controlling me any longer. He did it long enough to me.

I actually had a smile on my face when I went down for breakfast the next morning noticing for the first time, everyone had smiled back at me. I was going to try this "new me way" day by day hoping it works. Breakfast was delicious as always, and I let Maria know that it was. I actually could taste everything I put in my mouth, too.

I was invited to a Halloween party by friends of Aunt Sandy a few days ago that I quickly declined, but after several minutes of considering my invite, I thought I just might go after all. I had told Aunt Sandy I wasn't interested in going when we were first invited, but the new me was wanting to go now. Aunt Sandy was elated to hear this, and we began to discuss our costumes almost immediately. It would do me good to be around other people, I thought. No one would know who we were, if we didn't want to remove our masks, and I planned to stay anonymous as long as I could. I could feel safe that way. Safe from them knowing it was me, and safe from having to talk to anyone I didn't want to, and yet be in my own comfort zone.

Aunt Sandy and I arrived, and I thought maybe I had made a mistake in coming, but thought it would be really rude of me to just leave. After a few minutes I was actually having a remarkably great time, which really surprised me. I was able to recognize most of the people when they spoke, but they were baffled at who I could be. Except for this one person. I could tell it was male from the body structure, but it was obvious he didn't want to be recognized either, by having a voice modifier which made it difficult. I'm not sure what he was suppose to be, other than a swamp creature from the black lagoon, or something else creepy looking, but that was fine with me. I was safe, yet had an enjoyable conversation with "him".

The two of us laughed it up several times over his corny jokes, and even made small talk on things in general. I was intrigued by this mysterious man wondering whom ever it might have been. Neither of us was willing to reveal who we were, which was perfectly fine with me. Finally, I excused myself, and went inside to look around once more before making my exit, as the party was dwindling down.

I thanked the hostess saying she had a fantastic turn out, and I had enjoyed it very much. I went to the car to wait for Aunt Sandy to come out when she was ready. I was in no hurry myself, but I thought I might be able to find out who that swamp creature thing was as he left, but I didn't. I was intrigued now, as I did have a great time, and enjoyed talking to him. Somebody would know who he was, you'd think.

Aunt Sandy came out of the house bubbling over what a great party it was, and asked if I enjoyed myself. I said I had, and she was pleased to hear that. She had kept her eyes on me throughout the night making sure I wasn't holed up in some corner by myself.

Leave it to Aunt Sandy to do just that. Relieved when I was mingling with the people, and making my way around, to enjoy the night. She asked if I had met any ghouls or goblins I wanted to talk about. I didn't tell her about the swamp creature. I wasn't ready to discuss men with anyone yet. But yet, I felt she knew who it was, but not offering that vital information to me.

I told her the party was nice, and it made me think about all the Halloween parties that were held at our house when I was growing up. I think Aunt Sandy enjoyed scaring us kids as much as she possibly could. The covered pavilion outside was decorated perfect for the bewitching parties, with bales of hay to sit on, to the many stuffed scarecrows tied to the posts to prevent anyone from running into them, and possibly getting hurt. She had everything there to scare the dickens out of us. The eerie music could be heard the moment my friends got out of their cars, and continued throughout the party. Gooey things we would place our hands into, to the many other ways to win a prize. The weather was always creepy, dark, and with a wind that would kick up at the perfect time adding to the excitement. What great fun Aunt Sandy had made for me. A piece of my life I hadn't thought much about until now, and realized I had missed out on having fun for a long time.

On our drive home, I wished I had found out who held my attention for most of the party. I enjoyed talking, and listening to him, that I could kick myself for not finding out anything more about him. Someone had to have known, and I could probably ask around to find out. Until I do I will have to just be glad for the wonderful night I did have.

SHOW DOWN

O ur hunters were to arrive at the resort within the next few days. I kept myself busy by helping to prepare their cabins with Aunt Sandy. There were only eight guys coming this year, and they booked the two largest cabins for the entire week. I remembered how much fun they had been when I was still living at home. They were loud, and totally obnoxious at times when they came back from dinner. Aunt Sandy said it was the "spirits" doing it to them. What little did I understand exactly what spirits she was referring to at that time.

I didn't know what type of work they did, as their hands didn't show any signs of callus spots, but I knew it had to be good work if they could afford these hunting trips every year. They always tipped us very well when they left, which they didn't need to, but I didn't mind. Even little ole me got a large tip for being a big help to my aunt.

Every time they were lucky enough to get a deer or two, they would give Aunt Sandy a portion of it for us to enjoy. I never enjoyed it. All I could think about was the beauty of the deer, and the movie Bambi. I would rather eat sawdust off the floor than eat any deer meat. Not my cup of tea by any means, but Aunt Sandy loved it. She'd make most of it into jerky that she would share with the others while watching a football game. I stuck to my potato chips and french onion dip, over eating any deer. The guys also would donate the rest to the local homeless shelter, which I thought was very kind of them. Aunt Sandy said they were the kind of hunters that just enjoyed the sport, but not the rewards.

When the hunters were out doing their thing in the woods across the street, Aunt Sandy had me and Tommy gather all the Adirondack chairs up that would need to be sanded or scuffed to repaint while the weather still held up. The days were still warm but the nights were down right cold now. I loved scrapping the chairs for some reason. I would turn the radio on to a great rock and roll station, and start sanding and scrapping away. It made the time fly by, and enjoyable. It didn't make it seem like a long dredging chore either by listening to the music.

Phillip never liked to listen to music of any kind, and made it difficult for me to enjoy it. Tommy loved the same music as I did, and we had small talks now and then, between songs, but it was really strained between us. When I wanted to talk, he would pull away, or if the topic wasn't what he wanted to talk about, he quickly changed it. Several times I caught him just looking at me. I have to admit, it sent shivers through my body like it had before when we were teenagers.

Tommy and I were busy in the garage prepping the chairs when Maria came running out of the house looking frantic. She was holding my cell phone in her hand, and a look of heavy concern across her face, which told me something serious must be wrong. Maria never made it her business to answer my cell phone so this was very unusual.

Tommy and I stopped sanding on the chairs immediately, and I asked her if everything was alright. Tommy had muted the radio so we were able to speak without shouting. She informed me Elizabeth had been calling nonstop for the past half hour, so she thought it might be important, and took the call this time.

Maria handed me the phone just as it had started ringing again. It was Elizabeth calling. I answered immediately and could tell Elizabeth was winded, and needed to talk to me immediately. She kept her voice down low saying she didn't want to be overheard because she was sitting at her desk at the bank where anyone could possibly hear the conversation. Apparently, Phillip was in a rage, and was on his way to see me. Word got out about him over charging all his clients, and a big audit was starting to find all the discrepancies in the files from some very important people. Somehow, or should say someone, leaked that information, and fraud investigators had been informed. It had been in all the papers, including the TV. Phillip was in deep hot water, and he was seeking out who the whistle blower could be to make sure that was the end of it. I know I didn't leak it out to any authorities, but heaven forbid what he would do if he found that person that had leaked it. Elizabeth was worried on what he was going to do to me. I assured her I had nothing to do with it, and planned on telling Phillip so, if he did show up at the resort.

Long story short, he thought for sure it was me getting back at him for everything he had done, and he was on his way to see me to find out why I would do that to him, and try to incriminate me with it. He thinks I was the one who turned him in when I hadn't said a word to anyone, other than Aunt Sandy and Maria. I knew my aunt wouldn't have turned him in because it probably would have dragged me into his mess, and she didn't want that for me. Not that Aunt Sandy or Maria wouldn't have wanted to, I'm sure, but they knew enough to keep their distance from him for my sake.

Elizabeth had called to warn me about Phillip coming here, the "last place on earth that he would ever set foot in again," as he told me several times after being here that one and only weekend. Elizabeth thought I needed a heads up that he was in an out of control rage like no one around him had ever seen before. She felt he was dangerously out of control and was worried about my safety.

Elizabeth also informed me that several people had turned their notice in to leave their position at the bank, and Phillip didn't even give them a chance to finish out their allotted time. They had been escorted immediately to the door. Many had planned ahead, and had all their personnel stuff already out of their office, knowing Phillip wouldn't be happy. And he wasn't. He told them he would do everything in his power to see that they would never find another job in the banking industry. Phillip was ruthless, cruel, and he knew he had power. Little did he know that most of them already had another job lined up, and didn't need his reference anyhow.

I wasn't shocked Phillip would think it had been me to turn him in, but it wasn't. When I first left the bank I had thought about it, but decided it was better that I didn't have anything more to do with him in any shape, or form. I had put him in the past, and wanted it to remain that way.

No sooner had I got off the phone with Elizabeth and started working on the chairs, I saw the limo pulling into the driveway, followed by our hunters walking back from their afternoon of hunting. I was really getting worried of what Phillip would do to me, let alone say to me. I stood where I knew I could escape if I had to get away from Phillip as he got out of the limo.

I quickly composed myself greeting him with a cold "hello", and asked what he was doing here. Phillip was in a rage, just like Elizabeth described, and made it to the garage in as few giant steps as possible. Tommy came up to my side asking if I wanted him to leave. I shook my head no, as Phillip began his yelling, and I was glad Tommy stayed right beside me. Obviously, Phillip didn't care who was there anyhow as he puffed his chest out to show he was in control of the situation, not realizing he was making a total ass out of himself.

I stood my ground allowing him to yell as long as he wanted, and as loud as he felt was necessary. Maria quickly left to go inside the house. He had the attention of our hunters as well by then, and it just fueled Phillip more, because he had an audience. Phillip's accusations were totally ridiculous, as I calmly told him. I had no clue what he was talking about. I hadn't done any reporting to any authority, but in hindsight I should have, for all the deceit he had done to the clients at the bank. I also reminded him he had told me to keep my mouth shut about what went on in the office, if I wanted to stay working there, which I had at that time anyhow, glad I wasn't working there now. I was spilling the beans on him in front of everyone now, and they were definitely listening to the whole ugly story.

Phillip called me an ungrateful disgruntle employee out to destroy him. That was when I said I wasn't taking revenge, nor was I a disgruntle employee. I was completely done with him the moment after I had caught him in our bed with Heather Jenkins, and was fired on the spot as I had been. I knew our so-called engagement was a farce leaving him to his own pathetic demons. Our relationship was over, and it wasn't going to be mended under no circumstance.

The only things I have from my office are the things that belonged to me, nothing else that he was accusing me of taking. Apparently, he couldn't find any files he needed, but they were still there, if he or his new assistant, Heather, bothered to look. But, when you are clueless to where things are placed, you wouldn't know that either. Everything had been done for him, and he never had to lift a finger himself.

After what seemed like forever listening to his ranting, he turned toward me, poking his finger into my chest, informing me that going up against him would be bad, or a career ending decision, because he was taking me to court, to sue me for every penny I ever made there, and then some. He would destroy my pathetic little life leaving me penniless, and hopefully homeless.

That was when Tommy chimed in stating I had an attorney who had witnessed his accusations, threats, and assault. Phillip scuffed at him calling him a two bit hick attorney, but one by one, each hunter stepped forward saying they would be glad to represent me as well. Not only were they attorneys, but two of them were also judges. Phillip eyes grew huge with anger as his face turned the most scarlet red I had ever seen. Phillip was really enraged by everyone willing to help me, and finally left with his last warning to me that I better watch my back, as he got into his limo and left.

My knees were shaking so hard, and my heart was beating so fast I could feel it thumping in my ears on every beat. I actually collapsed onto the ground moments later. When I woke up, I was on the couch in the house with everyone around me. Tommy was wiping my face with a cool damp cloth. I just started crying because of the embarrassment of Phillip's visit, and that he had made such a horrible scene in front of everyone. They all knew now about me catching him in bed cheating with Heather, and what he had done about cheating several clients. Phillip had ratted himself out in front of everyone, and still tried to shift the blame onto me.

Tommy spoke up first to comfort me, and put his arm around me telling me not to worry about anything. What Phillip had done was fraud, and if it holds up in court, and he was found guilty, that was his own doing. He was the only one to benefit by it. He was the only one to blame. The hunters assured me Phillip wouldn't win if he even followed through on his accusations, and all of them said they would be there to help me, if I needed them. They could easily be called as witnesses to Phillip's threats, accusations, exposing what he had done, as well as poking his finger into my chest the way he did making it an assault. I heard them tell Tommy they would help him with anything he needed, to just give them a call. Phillip was guilty on many things, and they couldn't believe he tried pinning it on me.

I assured them that I was not the whistle blower. I did tell them I had flash drives of all the projects I worked on, and I had placed an encrypted memo that the projects were my work, and solely my work. No one else was involved with the presentation reports. I was the only person that had worked worked on them. I am so glad I had done that encrypting, and no one seemed to have noticed it either. I just thank my professors for that idea!

I thanked them all for wanting to help, as each one of them gave me their business cards to hold on to, just in case Phillip had the audacity to follow through on his threats. I was totally drained mentally and physically by then, and was glad when sleep over came me as they each left shortly.

Tommy and Maria were really concerned for me, and what Phillip had threatened. Maria had called the sheriff to get him off the property when she had gone inside the house when Phillip arrived, but they didn't arrive in time to see or hear anything spewing out of Phillip's mouth. Wish the sheriff had arrived on time and removed Phillip off the property, because a police report would have to have been made then. I think I had enough people there to witness what Phillip had said to me anyhow, without a police report.

A New Beginning

O nce the hunters had left that weekend, Aunt Sandy and I cleaned the cabins washing everything the following day. All the Halloween decorations were taken down, and packed away until next year. They were mostly the lighted plastic jack-o-lanterns Aunt Sandy had on the porch steps, the ghosts, bats and spiders scattered around the yard. The rest could remain where they were until after Thanksgiving because they were just autumn leaves, adding several turkeys, and a cornucopia to the decor.

Aunt Sandy was wanting to talk as soon as I felt up to it. She had heard all about Phillip's visit, and wasn't pleased he had shown up like he did. She wished she had been there to give him her boot in the ass that he deserved and tossed off her property. I could just vision her doing so, too.

After lunch we grabbed a glass of iced tea settling in the sun room where it was nice and toasty warm. She had asked

Tommy and Maria to join us as they were witness to the whole escapade yesterday, if I didn't object. I was fine with that because they needed to hear the whole ugly truth of Phillip, his banking practices, and the treatment I received, as well as his clients.

I explained everything to them, especially how Phillip had put the fear of God in me about not saying a word about the unethical practices Phillip had been doing. I was living in a city I knew nothing much about, except for it being a large busy city, or what I had read in books, and knew I was engaged to a very powerful and conniving man. I even told them how I had worked hours upon hours on his presentations without getting any recognition for it. I also told them of my encryption on each and every single project, while I was at it. That was just the beginning of me bearing my soul. I was unappreciated as a human and didn't realize it, until I left the city and Phillip behind.

I explained my presentation reports weren't just a few papers put together haphazardly talking about our business, and what we could offer to each client. I researched every client's purpose of them banking with us. Depending on the reason they wanted the loan, I had it there for them. Every presentation report had a list of regulations and restrictions ordered by the state, land terrain, climate, air quality, projected time frame, list of highly qualified company references they could count on in their area, charts on everything they would need, and anything else they would possibly need was all in my report. Maybe the presentation reports were too well prepared, but that was what my position was at the bank. I wanted to do the best presentation for Phillip to possibly, woo the clients our way. I had all the information tucked neatly in a binder for each person present at the meeting. The research would take many long tedious hours, but it was always worth it when they chose our bank to go with. Guess that was the only pride and appreciation I got for the work I had done.

I told them I found out that Phillip was over charging each client, such as charging for advising them on their accounts, when he never even spoke with them. The clients had someone else taking care of the bills in their offices, and they never questioned it, just paid the bill. The more he got away with it, the more often he did it, and how it made me feel when I saw what he had done on the client's accounts. He didn't have to make false charges. He was already making a huge profit from all these accounts.

Phillip had told me to keep my mouth shut, and I did. Don't know if it was the control he had over me, or just out of fear of being rejected by him. Either way, it was wrong, so I started documenting everything with notes on my personal laptop daily. A laptop that was mine, and mine alone. I never used it any where, but in my apartment, for fear of being found out, and had it placed in a secure spot in case Phillip ever came over. I was tormented by my love for Phillip, and the guilt of what I should have done from the start. I had to live with that, and be the sole person burdened with that secret.

It was so embarrassing for me to spills the beans. When I thought I didn't have any more tears to shed and I thought I had finished, I had more to say and more tears to shed. I had been embarrassed, humiliated, made a fool of, chewed up, spit out, leaving me now with mistrusted feelings towards men, and the lack of self confidence I once had in myself, just evaporated. Poof, gone. My heart had been ripped out of my chest leaving me feeling hollow on life itself.

When I got on the topic about catching him with Heather, Maria clasped her hands over her mouth. Tommy was gritting his teeth so hard his jaw line was clearly ruggedly stiff. He was seething, I could tell. Aunt Sandy had her mouth open shaking her head from side to side, and her eyes watered up. It was painful talking about it, I felt like a second rated lover of Phillip's, and not his fiance. I finished telling them the whole ordeal while I bowed my head down in shame.

They all sat there as I blubbered out my last five years of my career, and the wonderful life I thought I had. Several times I could see my pain in their eyes, and the red madness in their expressions as I talked. I wasn't looking for their sympathy or anything, but I knew they needed to know the whole ugly truth now, since Phillip had made such a scene at our house, and most of it had been exposed.

Aunt Sandy wasn't there to witness the scene, but from what everyone had informed her when she returned from her shopping, she was furious. The hunters sat her down telling her they were there witnessing the whole ugliness, and that they were there to support us in any way they could, before they departed. Aunt Sandy appreciated that from them.

I was a broken person. I didn't think I could ever recover from the devastation and blow to myself that I have felt since that day I was fired. I needed their help, support, and love to gain back the respect I had for life, and for myself. I needed it now more than ever. I was spiraling downhill at a rapid rate again, and it wasn't good.

They had questions they wanted answered which I obliged

to each, and every one of them, with some being harder and more embarrassing than others, to answer. Aunt Sandy had the most, and I was surprised with the ones Tommy asked of me. They were all concerned wanting me know they had my back, and would help me with anything I need to become whole again. They wanted me to know they understood and loved me no matter what.

Tommy said I sure didn't deserve to be treated as bad as I had been. As Maria and Aunt Sandy got up to leave, they gave me an assuring hug telling me how much they loved me, and will do the best they could to help me through this mess. I really needed that. They walked out of the room together when Tommy came up to hug me. It was the most gentle hug, as he whispered he would have never treated me that way, asking if he could please help me in any way, to be the Lexi he once knew, and loved so much. He wanted time for me to process everything that had happened, but would like to talk one on one with me when I felt up to it again. All I could do was nod my head yes, as he hugged me once more before walking out of the room.

I sat back down on the chair I had been in and it felt as if the whole burden had been lifted off my shoulders, and I would be able to go forward with my life, without any secrets or misgivings on how I was feeling, and why I was feeling the way I was. I was transparent now, and had a heart that desperately needed mending.

I knew it is going to be a long process for all of us, especially for me, and I can only hope I can be happy with myself again. I have my support team here knowing I can trust them with my bad days, as much as my good days. On my bad days everyone there would understand why, and either give me my space, or just encourage me if they could, to feel better.

It was a start, a new start for me and I was ready to do it without any misgivings.

CLEARING
THE AIR

D ays started to get shorter with the temperatures dropping just about as fast. The sky was mostly overcast daily only allowing the sun to appear for brief periods of time. Nights were down right cold and with the dark skies, it took on a sinister look of what could be waiting ahead. Thanksgiving was quickly approaching. Most of the resorts along the beach had closed for the year and would remain closed, until the next season. If there were people traveling through the town just wanting to stay the night somewhere, Aunt Sandy would open the cabins for them without batting an eye. It wasn't often that happened, but they were welcomed for whatever reason, and Aunt Sandy always invited them to join us at the house for a hot meal. For the most part, the resort was semi-closed until the summer, but there are times when a person was just too tired to travel on any further or not feeling well. Aunt Sandy knew it was going to be hard to find a place open this time of year to sleep, so a little work on her behalf to open up a cabin, was nothing.

Reservations would soon start to come in for the summer months, and I'd book them for the people until we were full. We would get a sense of how busy we were going to be by the time spring came around. So many people were regulars customers coming up every summer year after year. We looked forward to their arrival and considered them part of our extended family. Many times they would bring other people with them making the cabins availability fill up quickly. Word of mouth was the best advertising a person could get, and it was free. It has worked all these years for us. It also was a great indication of how we were running the business. No one ever batted an eye when we finally had to raise the rental costs due to our own costs, but no one seemed to mind. They were just happy to get a unit and looked forward to their stay on the beach.

Maria called us in for a meeting late one afternoon after we had finished working outside on some little projects Aunt Sandy needed done. Since we didn't have much going on with the rentals, Aunt Sandy had Maria coming in for only a few hours a day to cook and do the cleaning in the house.

Maria wanted to go over the holiday meal that she always prepared for us. It sounded delicious as she went through the list she planned to cook, and as always, she would be joining us, as well as her husband Fred, for the day. That was a tradition with us, that had been carried on since Maria started working for Aunt Sandy, which seemed like forever ago.

Mom and I spent most of the holidays with Aunt Sandy. It was a shorter time at Thanksgiving because we only had a long weekend, but other times like Christmas, we stayed a week. Maria was part of our family back then too.

I came in exhausted after working in one of the cabins all day with Tommy, giving the knotty pine walls a fresh coat of shellac, to find Maria had baked a variety of pies. The aroma was breath taking as soon as the door was opened, and my taste buds were at attention. I noticed she made an extra pumpkin pie for us to enjoy before Thanksgiving, and had that set aside from the others. She knew us very well and knew if she hadn't baked it, we would have swiped one of the pies from the shelf she had the others setting on for Thanksgiving!

The turkey was already thawing in the sink and supplies for her homemade stuffing were on the counter in the butler pantry, lined up in her order. I was looking forward to Thanksgiving dinner this year, and even watching the football game after dinner with everyone.

I hadn't heard another word from Phillip since that day he came to the resort, but I was expecting anytime I would. Either from him directly, or from one of his attorneys. Until that happens, he was put on the back burner of my mind, the best I could anyhow. I didn't need to worry about him, my back was covered from Tommy and the hunting friends we had. I was moving on and had learned my lesson on being used or controlled by a man.

I had called Elizabeth a couple of times since Phillip was here, thanking her for the heads up. It helped me compose in my head what I had planned to tell him when he arrived. She was in the process of finding a different job herself because of everything going on at the bank. She felt it was only a matter of time when the doors would be closed, locking everyone out. The auditors had found all the over charged items on their own during their investigation, and it wasn't looking good for Phillip at all. No one seemed to know who the whistle blower was, but I assured Elizabeth it wasn't me. Elizabeth felt it could have been someone that left the bank shortly after I had, in the payroll department or a teller even. However, Elizabeth didn't want to be caught without any income coming in knowing if they closed the bank, there wouldn't be a pay check that week. She placed her applications in other states hoping for a change, and to be out of New York completely. I totally understood that, and couldn't blame her for that either.

She wasn't too surprised at all about the scene Phillip had made here, but when I told her of all the attorneys and two judges that witnessed it all, she let out a war hoop loud and clear. She felt as I had, that Phillip stepped out of his control zone and into a wasp nest of problems. She was glad they were all here and willing to support me, if I needed them. She even offered to testify herself if I wanted her to. I already knew she would be receiving a subpoena when the time came. She knew the long hours I put in at the bank, at home, that the presentation reports were all mine, and she also knew of what Phillip had been doing all along, too. She was ready for the day she would have to testify.

Heather was still with Phillip supporting his every move and defending him with everything like only a puppet would do, but how much longer was the question everyone was asking. Rumor has it she just found out she was pregnant, which Phillip was none too happy about. I don't suppose he would be. He didn't want a family or any kid touching anything that was his, getting their filthy little fingerprints all over everything. Selfish, self-centered, and definitely not a good role model at all for a child to have to live through. There was tension felt in the air all the time Phillip and Heather were together. Elizabeth said it was just a matter of time before Phillip dumps her.

I told her they ought to get a pool going in the office as to when that would happen. For both parts, the baby's birth and when she would be let go from working there. We both burst out in laughter at that thought. Heck, I might even enjoy that myself! I told Elizabeth to put me in for ten dollars.

I did feel bad for the baby though, if Heather and Phillip stayed together. It would be hard on the child living under those conditions and a severed relationship right from the beginning from Phillip.

With Heather being pregnant and things not going so grand between her and Phillip, I thought she deserved every bit of what she was facing. I thought about it for awhile before I actually felt sorry for her and knew she was going to be a single parent totally on her own, especially if Phillip was hauled off to prison for everything he had been doing illegal at the office.

Phillip had to actually hire a few new employees right away, because many of his old employees had left suddenly, without much notice given. Everyone of the newbies were young, beautiful, just out of college, and every single one was a female. A way to control and mold them into what he expects from them right from the start. More than likely, a man would have noticed things where Phillip had felt that most women were blind to everything. It was his charisma that he would use, and the young women wouldn't know any different. Go figure!! Phillip would work his charm on them right from the beginning, as he had done me. He would have control over them, hook, line and sinker. They were now caught in his web not knowing what they were getting themselves into. I know a leopard doesn't change its spots and yet, I kind of felt sorry for them at the same time.

Maybe I was being cynical, because of what had happened to me, but that was how I felt. I don't think anything is ever going to change my opinion on that either. Some people have to learn life the hard way, and I surely fell into that category.

Tommy and I hadn't had our talk yet, that he asked about when I bared my soul that day and I was rather glad he wasn't pressuring me into doing it. He has been so kind helping me with everything, always giving me praise for my work and also for my appearance, which I thought was pleasantly nice. Said I was getting my glow back which he felt was a good sign. I even started to notice my appearance had improved the past few weeks. I quit living in sloppy clothes that barely hung on to me from them being over-sized. I don't know if its because of Tommy or not, but I was feeling better about it myself again.

Aunt Sandy hasn't been her bubbly self the past few weeks. I know it can't be money she's worried about because she did very well this past summer. Since I do her books, that was my way of knowing that little tidbit, but whatever it was, it wasn't my business to question her about it. Maybe the winter gloom has set in for her with the cloudy skies day after day lately, but regardless, I am going to keep an extra eye out on her. I told Tommy about my concerns, and he immediately offered to help me by keeping an eye on her as well. I think Maria knows what's going on, because I have caught them talking extra quietly several times in the kitchen lately when they hadn't heard me come in the door. I sure hope it isn't over me and Phillip. She doesn't need to worry about that. I think it will be handled, and over soon.

In the meantime, we were all busy doing things around the resort that keep us occupied, and time was going by fast. Things will settle down once we get the cabin walls done, and we will be able to relax for a few weeks.

I enjoyed the down time because Aunt Sandy, and I, would be able to chat more often, and she was always buying new jigsaw puzzles for us to work on, many hours of playing cards and watching movies we hadn't had time for during the summer months. We had many books to read that had to be put off until now. I could picture us just reading by the fireplace burning logs, sipping on hot chocolate, and wrapped in one of Aunt Sandy's afghans. I couldn't wait!

It would also give us time to reorganize plans for the summer activities, tweaking them to perfection. I would be in charge of that chore and ordering supplies we would need in advance. So, we really didn't just sit around doing nothing or wasting the time away. There were things for us to do for the resort, but not on a fast pace schedule like we had when the resort was fulling open for our guests.

Thanksgiving dinner was just as I expected, delicious in every way. Maria outdid herself again with all the food she had prepared. Leftovers were going to last the rest of the month for us! I sure didn't mind that one bit either. Nothing better than a cold turkey sandwich at midnight to hit the spot. Aunt Sandy always insists on Maria taking several plastic wares full of leftovers home with her for her and Fred to enjoy later in the week.

When we finished eating our feast, we settled in the living room for the annual football game, cheering the teams on as if we were right there in the stadium watching them play in person. High fives and booing were loud, and easy flowing from all of us. I had a marvelous time, and for the first time in years, content with how my holiday had been.

We always talked during the dinner about what was up in our lives, and any new plans we had. Just normal talk, and a lot about the football game, which was always a good spirited conversation. For me, I just said about my situation with Phillip ending with the famous statement, "no news was good news", and with all the problems concerning Phillip, I just hoped he would just forget about me. I also said how happy I was being back home, feeling great, feeling safe, and with all the love and support I had been given, I couldn't be thankful enough. I thanked everyone for it, and looked forward to a refreshed outlook on life.

In New York I did nothing but work. I missed celebrating the holidays, and I did not look forward to them either knowing I'd be working through them anyhow, and usually by myself. Well, I was working, I don't know what Phillip was doing, but he was gone most of the day. Many times I would run down to a little cafe after Phillip was gone to enjoy a turkey dinner. Not many places were open on Thanksgiving, but I was glad I could count on this place being open all the time. Not many people were eating there, but they also probably didn't have anyone to spend the holiday with either, or have someone to prepare a nice meal for them. How sad that was and then I realized I was just as bad off as they were. I always made sure to compliment on the meal and leave a hefty size tip before leaving to go back home.

Tommy and I sat up to watch a movie after the game was over, after everyone had left. Aunt Sandy already had gone to bed. She seemed to be feeling better lately, but that might have been because her Packers was the game on TV, and they won the game. The perfect day for her. So, whatever had been nagging at her, must have been resolved.

Tommy and I enjoyed another slice of Maria's wonderful pies as we watched the movie. I loaded my pumpkin pie slice with whip cream as high as I could, and all around the pie as well. I didn't have anyone make me feel guilty for the amount I had squirted on. Tommy laughed at it, asking if there was any pie under it all. It felt so nice to be able to relax and I was feeling happy.

Tommy asked if we could talk after the movie was over. I thought I was too sleepy. Actually, I was dreading that talk he wanted to have, but with Tommy wanting to talk was only right for me to stay awake longer. He hadn't pressured me all this time for that talk. I thought I was ready for it, but I would have preferred to have gone to bed.

We discussed many general topics at first, which I thought was a good way to lead into it by breaking the ice on whatever I knew he wanted to talk about. We made the deal I could ask him anything as well, and I did. I had many questions I needed answers to. My big question I wanted an answer to I couldn't ask yet, but I want to know why he never wrote to me the entire time I was in college. That question didn't seem appropriate at this time. Once we started talking, it became easier for me to open up to him on myself and I really think he felt the same way. We had many years to get caught up on, and it actually turned out to be a pleasant time discussing things with him.

I learned a few things I didn't know about him, and what he had done after I left for college. He had come to New York a few times with the hopes to see me, to hopefully have dinner one night, but when he did, he got cold feet, or saw me with Phillip. He couldn't intrude on me then because I was already spoken for. He thought I looked tired each time, not having the glow I used to have. He didn't feel I was happy there, but he also knew he couldn't expect me to talk to him or leave with him to come back home. Several times he would just watch me through the window of the bank as I worked at my desk from across the street, or when I was pulling away in a cab, or the company limo.

He could never understand why I wouldn't return home after college, thinking maybe he had done something wrong to keep me away. I didn't have the heart to tell him I needed to prove to myself that I was worthy of receiving that scholarship like I had, and to show my aunt I had it in me to be successful. I knew my aunt was proud of me, as she has said so many times, but she wanted me to have a chance she never had, living on my own and away from parent figures. To have the adventures I could tell my kids about later in life and be happy I had that opportunity with no regrets.

Tommy asked if I ever thought about him and I couldn't lie. I told him at first I missed him terribly, but after my third year away from home, things started to shift, and I absorbed myself into my studies. I hadn't heard from him thinking he had moved on with his life, and I was a thing in the past. It was true that I had moved on, but it wasn't without many thoughts of him, and what we had when we were together. He was my first love and I didn't want to change that by any means, but once I was hired at the bank, with Phillip having me in his arms things changed so fast. I wasn't sure what I wanted. Even though I thought I was in love with Phillip, it wasn't the same kind of love I had felt for Tommy. He understood completely what I was telling him.

I asked Tommy if he had moved on himself. H e said he had gone to college, passed the bar exam becoming an attorney, to also had to prove he was worthy as well. He thought that was why I didn't come back home to see him, because he wasn't what I longed for in my life anymore. He was heartbroken the entire time and just settled for the fact he had lost me completely. Finally, he decided he would just settle with his life at the resort. Whenever Aunt Sandy spoke about me, a piece of his heart was ripped away. He went away for a year traveling all over, but thought of me the entire time. He finally decided to just come back to the resort and started working again, as if he had never left.

When his grandfather passed away it was a deep blow to him, as it was to Aunt Sandy, but when he was asked to stay on to help my aunt and he was grateful for that. She was the only person he had left in his life that had been family to him.

When he saw me pull into the driveway when I came home that day, I had lifted his spirits. He wanted to run over to me to give me the biggest hug known to mankind, but he knew he had to stay his distance until the right time came along.

I couldn't believe we talked getting the air cleared on all our feelings and things made more sense to me later that night, actually early morning hours would be more precise, when I was laying in bed thinking, and thanking my lucky stars how wonderful things were now. I thought how blessed I am being here with everyone once again. Yes, I had a lot to be thankful for this year, and I was going to cherish it with all my might.

'TIS THE SEASON

I was not able to get up as quickly as everyone else the next morning, but once I smelled the coffee brewing, and bacon frying, I was awake and starving. I bounced around the corner of the kitchen just as Tommy was about to sit down. He greeted me with his broad smile asking if I slept well last night. I amazingly had slept great, and felt as if I was ready to conquer the day.

There were things that were on my to-do list I had made the day before that needed to be done. All the decorations from autumn had to come down, be packed, stored, and replaced with all the Christmas decorations. I loved Christmas and was really excited to get these decorations out. Little did I know, Tommy had all the autumn items already down and packed away, with as many totes of Christmas items down from the attic, and ready to work on in the garage, as soon as we were done with breakfast.

Aunt Sandy had lights galore to string on the house, evergreen trees, and along the driveway. Plenty of wooden figurines of nutcrackers, soldiers, a huge life sized nativity scene to put in the front yard, and I saw she had new wreaths for the front of the door and windows. Her place was transformed into a winter wonderland every year. She loved it when people would drive by just to look at her display. Several times she would go out to greet them at the road, serving them hot chocolate and powdered donuts, as they stood by their cars taking pictures. She relished in making people happy.

Breakfast was lighthearted, and the three of us just sitting there talking and joking around about what we have heard or read about lately, or something we had done in the past. It was so enjoyable to be there, and in on the laughs once again. As soon as breakfast was over I grabbed my coat, put my boots on, and flew out the door to start the decorating.

Tommy was already outside when I got there. He was up earlier, and got busy so we wouldn't waste any time putting up the Christmas decorations. He loved Christmas as much as Aunt Sandy and I, and couldn't wait to get started.

Once Aunt Sandy came out with her diagram of where everything was to be placed, we began our quest. Tommy was an expert on the lights putting them on the house quickly, as if he had been doing it all his life. Come to think of it, he has. He said he has placed them on the house for so many years now, he should have been able to do it blindfolded.

The new lighted wreaths for the door and windows were much larger this year, and were absolutely stunning. So much to do that the morning just flew by faster than what I thought. We took time off to quickly eat a cold turkey sandwich on homemade rolls slathered with mayonnaise. It hit the hunger spot, and as soon as I finished my sandwich and chips, we went back outside to finish the display.

December was such a busy month for us, as we did a traditional Christmas party for friends, we also would visit the homeless shelter, shelter for battered women, and the group home for children, giving everyone in there a gift, and wishing them a Merry Christmas. Aunt Sandy dressed as Mrs. Claus with Tommy in the Santa suit. I will dress as an elf, if the costume still fits, as we embark on the shelters.

Aunt Sandy would order a few hundred items each year from a dollar store to pass out. The women received a small basket of items they were doing without, being in the shelter. Mostly body wash, powder, fluff bag for washing their dedicates, and other items she could find that they might like to receive. The kids received coloring books with coloring pencils, matchbox cars, stuffed animals, and of course a small box of candy. These were neatly stuffed in a red stocking. Everyone also received a pair of mittens, scarves, socks, and pajamas to unwrap. The shelters also received a food box to help with the holiday dinner for everyone. Aunt Sandy loved giving back to the community as much as possible.

I loved seeing the faces on the little kids when they received a gift from Santa, and knowing their little hearts were happy. It also gave me the feeling, as I'm sure Aunt Sandy felt herself, of doing a good deed. Remembering how it made us feel when we were younger to receive a gift to unwrap. It made us feel so happy to be able to give back. That was what I love about this holiday, the giving and joy it brought to others, and the feeling it brought to us.

Phillip would always buy me a special gift. Usually a piece of beautiful jewelry, but he would just hand it to me a few days earlier with a "Merry Christmas". He never bothered to have it wrapped either, because that was a waste in his eyes No tree was allowed in his place, and definitely no Christmas music played. He said it was bad enough he had to do it at the bank and he wasn't going to have it continue on to his house. He was gone most of the time on a "business" ski trip anyhow, so I was alone. He probably thought the piece of jewelry he gave me would make up for everything, but it only cheapened the whole holiday for me.

Because Phillip was gone, I would stay at my apartment where I did have a small tree in front of my window, and I did play Christmas carols to my heart content. He never bothered me there so he never knew what I had, or didn't have, for Christmas. My poor tree reminded me of a Charlie Brown Christmas tree, but like in that movie, it was beautiful! I could fit the tree, the small string of lights, and few ornaments, all inside the tree box nice and neatly, to use again the next year.

I decorated my bedroom with that little tree the other night, and for the first time that tree looked more beautiful than ever. We were both in a happy, and safe place, and it seemed to have taken on a new happier feeling this year.

Aunt Sandy believed Christmas music started the day after Thanksgiving to put everyone in the Christmas mood. Several times I caught myself singing along with the music, and was glad no one had heard me as I looked around. Her favorite songs were the ones sung by Elvis Presley and Bing Crosby. What an odd mixture of music I thought to myself.

Tommy and I went to play pool every Friday night, and

it was great time being with friends. Betty, Barb, and Nancy were becoming great friends with me, and invited me to everything they had planned. The four of us went to the mall about an hour away together to shop on a Saturday, and have lunch making it a great girl's day out. We chatted nonstop all the way there, and all the way home. I learned more about them, and even a little more about Tommy on that drive. I was still not comfortable about talking about my past life, and kept the topic on the present, and what was going on at the resort.

I was able to complete my entire shopping for gifts that day, and was rather pleased with myself. I know Aunt Sandy will love her gift, as she has remarked a few times how she should buy one herself. The food processors were a big deal this year, and now she will have one. Plus the other smaller gifts I purchased for her.

Tommy was the hard one to buy for. I finally bought a pullover sweater, and watch for him. I overheard him tell one of the guys his watch finally bit the dust at the pool hall, and that gave me the idea. Maria and Fred were easy because they loved everything, and never buy anything they want when they should. Fred has this thing about saving every dime for their retirement. They will be getting a gift certificate for dinner at a restaurant they have always wanted to go to, and a stay at the hotel next to it overnight.

I learned that Tommy had tried to move on with his life over the years, but his dating was far and few in between. The new girls in his life never lasted long, according to Betty. They thought he was pining for someone he dated in high school that seemed to have broken his heart when she moved away. They never knew who she was, or any other information about it, but I knew, and I knew it had to be me. I didn't have the heart to inform them of that information either. It didn't sound like they were very happy with what that girl had done by leaving like she had, and they took Tommy's side on everything.

They thought it was so great that Tommy and I are together. And how happy he seemed to be lately, which made them happy for him. I stopped them right there telling them we aren't together as a couple like they thought, we're just good friends enjoying a night out together. They didn't believe that from what their husbands had told them. Apparently, Tommy was more open to his buddies than to me on his feelings.

I listened to every word they had to say on Tommy, and about his self destructive ways when he did things, as if he didn't care what life he had to offer anyone else, but to that girl who left him. I never thought of how my leaving had affected him, especially that bad.

Which made me wonder even more why he never wrote back to me. Was he that upset with me? Did he resent me leaving? And what did he think now? I professed my love to him in all my letters, and how it was going to be good for us when I finished college. For us!! But, it didn't seem like there was an "us" after receiving nothing back from Tommy during all that time.

If I brought any of this up with Tommy now, he will know who told me, and might shut his friends out of his life, which he needed them more than what he thinks. I didn't want that to happen. I was so perplexed on what to do or say when I got back home. He would be able to sense something was not right.

When I got home, no one was there so I quickly went in, and put the gifts under the tree. I had them wrapped at the mall so it was one less thing I would need to do. I noticed there was a gift under the tree for me, but it didn't say from whom. I picked it up shaking it, trying to figure out what it could be. It was small like maybe a bottle of perfume, but no liquid noise. Just as I was doing that, Tommy walked in laughing at me. He told me I was worse than a little kid trying to find out what was in a gift from Santa.

I quickly put the gift down, and threw the pillow off the couch at him. Then it began, the hardest hitting pillow fight ensued. I couldn't stop laughing, and as hard as I tried, I couldn't land a good hit on Tommy no matter what. He finally stopped when he had me pinned to the floor smiling that gorgeous smile of his. That was when we heard the back door open, and Aunt Sandy coming in. We sat up trying to look innocent as we could muster. My hair was such a tangled mess, and my shirt full of wrinkles. Aunt Sandy gave us the look of "what have you two been up to?" We burst into laughter, and threw a pillow at her too. It was now full throttle with the three of us hitting each other with a pillow. I hadn't had so much fun having a pillow fight since I was a kid. We were exhausted calling a truce to stop.

I think I dodged one that night, because I truly think Tommy was about to kiss me. I wasn't sure I would want him to kiss me, or even want him to stop, if he had kissed me.

Later that night I was laying in bed thinking about everything I had been through in my life, when I heard Tommy get up to use the bathroom. We had a Jack and Jill bathroom we shared between our bedrooms. My sliding door wasn't completely closed, and as soon as he flicked on the light, it drew my attention to the door. I wondered if he had remembered he shared that bathroom with me, because he never made sure my door was completely shut, and he was completely naked. I smiled to myself thinking all sorts of thoughts that I had of Tommy when we were kids, the things we did, the secrets we shared, and what I thought about him now. I quickly rolled over, and tried to fall asleep, but it was useless.

My little tree light lit my room nicely, and made me think of the times I had strung a string of lights around my ceiling to give the room some character. I chuckled how my aunt would tease me about them being up on a wall, and not on a tree. They were special to me, and I had the switch to change the colors on them to fit my mood, and to dim them when I wanted to. My room was alive with those lights shining on everything, and she never told me I had to take them down, which was the best part.

I thought about what the girls had said about Tommy earlier, and began to wonder if he still had the same feelings for me as he had when we were teenagers. Was I putting too much thought into what if it was true, and what I should do if it was, or if it wasn't. I don't know what time it was when I fell asleep, but I slept good, and was refreshed when I woke up.

As I was dressing, I noticed a little gift under my little tree from my "Secret Santa". It was a small candy cane with a ribbon tied around it. I had completely forgotten we do Secret Santa to everyone in the house before Christmas. I ran out later that day, and got a few things to leave around for Aunt Sandy, Tommy, and Maria. One of the things I always enjoyed doing with everyone, and cannot believe I forgot about it. Well, my candy cane was appreciated, and finding it under my little tree made it known to me it was from Tommy. My bedroom door was locked from the hallway, and the only way to my tree was through Tommy's room, through our shared bathroom.

I hurried downstairs for breakfast where I found another gift on my plate. It had to be from Aunt Sandy, because Maria wasn't there yet. These little gifts are always nice to get, and they are just little tokens of love and appreciation. This one was a new holiday scrunchie for my hair. It matched the sweater I was wearing, and I quickly put my hair into a pony tail using it.

Our day at the shelters went fabulous. Our friends showed up to help wrap everything the night before, which we thought was so thoughtful of them. We always could use extra hands doing these charities. We ordered several pizzas, and ate while we took a break. Aunt Sandy was happy to finally meet our friends we talked about often, and invited them to our Christmas party next week. They all said they'd attend and looked forward to it. It was going to be great, that I knew for a fact. Aunt Sandy didn't throw anything but great parties.

Tommy and I met up with all of them the next night to play pool, and exchanged a little gift with each other. When we pocketed a certain pool ball we got to go to the table a choose a wrapped gift. I was lucky to get a beautiful holiday candle that I would place on top of the mantle when we got home. Some others received candles as well, but I must admit, I thought mine was the prettiest of them all. There were some gag gifts on the table too, that we all busted a gut laughing when they were opened.

When we were done playing pool, and Tommy finished his last beer, we headed home. We promised Aunt Sandy we would decorate the many sugar cookies she had baked earlier, and was looking forward to it. Aunt Sandy bought every thing she could find to decorate the cookies making them elaborate. We also had to construct a gingerbread house which was a larger chore than what I ever remember it being.

Saturday was Aunt Sandy's Christmas party, and the house was quickly full of friends and family. Aunt Sandy loved to entertain, and this was the one time of the year she went all out making sure everyone would have a great time with plenty of food to fill their bellies. I wore a red velvet dress for this affair. As I walked into the room, Tommy looked over towards me, and just stared. Later that night after everyone left, he told me I was beautiful, and he had a hard time keeping his eyes off me. He was very good looking himself, and I was surely watching him as well. Several times Nancy would ask me if there was something I was looking at that I liked. I just smiled, and we both bust out laughing. I didn't need to speak any words, she knew.

After everyone had left I cleaned up the house for Aunt Sandy so she could rest. Tommy lent a hand in gathering all the dishes to the sink so I could load into the dishwasher. The party was a success, which I had no doubt it would be, and everyone seemed to have enjoyed it tremendously. I know I did, and to think all the years I didn't get the opportunity to have Christmas in New York like this, all because of Phillip.

He had a Christmas party every year, but that was the extent of celebrations. I was always so busy making sure everyone was well fed, and enjoying themselves, that I didn't have much of a celebration myself. I had to do all the planning for that from reserving the banquet room, decorations, food, appetizers, drinks and putting the bonuses inside the employees corporate Christmas cards. What did Phillip do…. NOTHING, but bask in the compliments he received for everything like he had done it all himself, just like with my presentation reports.

Heaven knows what they did this year, and who got stuck with that tedious detail. I didn't enjoy myself when Phillip was around. It was always about him, and he would make sure everyone's attention was drawn to the newest piece of jewelry he had given me that Christmas. Like he had to brag about how great he was to me. If only they all knew that he handed me the gift without even wrapping it, and wished me a Merry Christmas as he rushed out the penthouse door to a business night out.

I turned looking at the kitchen for the last time before making my way to the living room to watch a Christmas movie with Aunt Sandy, and Tommy. We had an old tradition of watching the same movie every Christmas season. Aunt Sandy always said traditions are what families are made of, and should be followed yearly to keep them alive. I can almost tell you word for word what the actors were saying without even looking at the screen. Having the larger TV made a big difference this year watching "A Miracle on 42nd Street". The colors were more vivid, and it sure beat the black and white TV we watched before.

One last trip to the kitchen to take our snack tray back before I headed upstairs. I was tired, and looking forward to my head hitting the pillow for some much needed sleep. I saw that Tommy had left his door open a little, and peeked in. He was humming a Christmas carol while wrapping another little gift. I was sure it would find it's way to my little tree by morning.

I dressed for bed, and after brushing my teeth, I was asleep faster than anyone else in the house, I'm sure. I slept hard, and before I knew it, it was time to get up. The little gift was under my tree like I suspected it would be, and I opened it quickly before getting dressed for breakfast. A tube of hand lotion that I knew was over the price limit we set to spend on these little gifts, but it was the brand that I loved to use. Tommy was being so thoughtful. I applied some on my hands as I made my way to breakfast.

SNOWSTORM

T his was going to be a hectic week at the stores, but I had a few things I needed to get for Aunt Sandy and Tommy, for their stockings hanging from the fireplace mantle. Simple things I should have purchased sooner, but put them off thinking I had plenty of time to do later. Guess it was the hustle and bustle of being in the stores at the last minute that I wanted to experience once again.

I ran into Barb and Betty at the store and we went to the café for lunch together. They were really happy to have been invited to our Christmas party raving on and on about that. There were several hints dropped that they could get use to that every year. I chuckled telling them I would be sure to invite them from now on, which they smiled over that news.

Betty remarked about how beautiful I looked that night, and how handsome Tommy looked, too. They noticed how much Tommy had his eyes on me the entire night bringing it to my attention. I reminded them once again we were just friends, but I think they knew better. I knew better, but not wanting to admit it yet myself. I was the happiest when I was around Tommy when we were working side by side. Told them if anything ever developed between us, I surely would inform them.

After lunch we parted our ways so we could finish our shopping and get home. We were all going to the New Years Eve party in town later in the week, and we would be seeing each other there. In the meantime, they were going to be busy with their families enjoying their time with them.

My last stop was to buy a handful of lottery tickets to put in the stockings and a gag gift for each. I was finally able to say I was done shopping and began to head for my car to go home. The traffic was absolutely horrible with everyone in a hurry and driving recklessly. Snow had started to fall again, I knew I really didn't want to be in town any longer myself with the snow accumulating as fast as it was. I hadn't drove in snow or on slippery roads for several years now and I could feel my car sliding from time to time. It was making me nervous knowing if I didn't get home soon, I would be in serious trouble. Didn't help matters that the sky was getting darker by the minute with the snow falling at such a rapid pace.

Just as I was about five miles from town, I saw Aunt Sandy and Tommy coming my way. They motioned for me to pull over as Tommy came running to my car. He said he would drive the rest of the way home for me, so I scooted over in the seat to let Tommy drive. I was never so glad to let him take the wheel. I would never admit to them that

I was worried about getting back home safely either. They knew I wasn't use to driving in these conditions anymore, and decided they better go looking for me right away. Aunt Sandy drove a head of us in her vehicle so we could be sure she got home safely as well. I decided not to drive again until Spring was here, and no more snow.

Tommy came over to let me out of the car once we were home, parking both cars in the garage. I was still shaking from the whole ordeal of driving and he put his arm around my waist to help me to the house. Once outside the garage my feet slipped out from under me because of the icy patch in the driveway. Tommy and I both tumbled to the ground. Once we realized we were on the ground we just looked at each other and started laughing. I thanked him for driving the rest of the way home before bursting into tears. I had more emotions right then than I have had in weeks and it was all because Tommy actually was concerned for my safety by coming to my rescue.

He said he was glad they were able to find me early enough so I wouldn't have to drive in the storm. They had heard of the storm developing fast on the TV and it was going to be furious storm. He wouldn't have wanted me to get stranded in a ditch or something, and was already headed to the car when Aunt Sandy caught up to him so they could find me.

We got up off the ground shaking the snow from ourselves and I hugged Tommy for thinking of me and my safety. We made it to the house without slipping, with a grip on each other to steady ourselves. Aunt Sandy asked if we had decided to make snow angels on the ground before coming in when she saw us. She had the biggest smile on her face so I knew she saw us on the ground. I smiled saying we were in the process of making a conjoined snow angel, and saw Tommy's face smile with several shades of red rising to his cheeks.

And what a snowstorm we did have! I could hear the wind howling fiercely outside my window during the night. I knew it was going to be a long drawn out storm from what the weatherman had said before I went to bed. Aunt Sandy suggested that I put an extra quilt on the bed, just in case we lose power during the night. The power did go out at sometime, and I just snuggled down deeper into my bed pulling the quilt up to my chin to stay warm. It helped for awhile, but then I was beginning to feel the cold seep in stealing my warmth from me. Tommy tapped on my door stating he started a fire in the fireplace, and the downstairs was pretty warm now, holding my slippers, and bathrobe, out to me. He had them downstairs by the fire getting them warm for me to slip into, knowing I would appreciate that. They were just wonderfully warm as I quickly put them on. Who does that for people other than Tommy? No one else I knew, that was for sure.

Aunt Sandy had made coffee over the fire in the fireplace which was hitting the spot. Tommy was getting himself ready to check on the generator, if it would kick on to get power to the house, and the cabins. Aunt Sandy was worried she'd have pipes busting in the cabins due to the storm, if we didn't attend to it as soon as possible.

Tommy got the generator going after several attempts, and in no time everything was getting back to normal. I offered to go to the cabins with Tommy to help, but he insisted we stay in the house where it was warm. I ran upstairs to grab a jogging outfit and socks out of my dresser, to warm by the fire so I could change into them as soon as they were warm. It was still comfortably warm in the living room, but I could feel the draft from the windows and door seeping in. It encouraged me to dress fast, and after nearly falling on the floor trying to pull my pants on, I was warm and toasty once again.

Aunt Sandy and I watched Tommy go into each cabin. When he came out of one, he'd give us a thumbs up, indicating everything was fine. I grabbed a mug of coffee for him to drink as soon as he came back into the house when he was done. He wasn't complaining at all, but remarked how bitterly cold it was with the wind blowing as hard as it was. Aunt Sandy said we would conserve the electric in the house all we could allowing the generator keep the cabins warm. I don't know if that was necessary to do but this was her business and livelihood out there with those cabins, and didn't question her.

Once Tommy warmed up he stoked the logs in the fireplace adding a few more logs to keep the house comfortably warm. We turned on the emergency radio Tommy brought up from the basement to listen to the news. The announcer stated that the storm decided to linger over our part of the country for the time being. There wasn't any chance of it moving out today or tomorrow either. He added to be sure pets were brought inside out of the harsh cold, and to check on our neighbors, friends, and the elderly to be sure they were all okay, if we could.

Aunt Sandy put her green paper in the window to let anyone passing by know we were fine, and her red paper with a white cross to let others know if they needed a place to stay until the storm passed, they would be welcomed here. I couldn't imagine anyone out there in this storm anyhow, but she always opened her house to stranded people regardless.

We didn't even see a snowplow drive by the house, and the drifts were higher than I ever had seen before. It was so quiet and peaceful outside, other than the howling wind now and then. Most of the windows had thick frost formed on them making it difficult to see out.

I planted my butt on the love seat closest to the fireplace with no plans to budge from that spot. I had a blanket wrapped around me with a good book to read to keep me occupied for awhile. I don't think I got very far into the book before I closed my eyes falling asleep. It was one of those type of days with everything dreary that makes me tired. I woke up to Tommy shaking me to tell me to eat something. I looked to him holding a plate for me. It had a grilled cheese sandwich on it, one of my favorite sandwiches in cold weather. He sat on the love seat next to me eating his grilled cheese sandwich sharing the bag of chips he brought in.

Aunt Sandy was asleep in her recliner across from us. She looked so tired and the sleep will do her good. She had been up so much during the night worried about the cabins until Tommy got the generator started. Tommy covered her with the blanket he was using so gently she never budged.

I opened my blanket up for Tommy to share with me, and he gladly scooted in next to me. As we sat there on the love seat he whispered to me he would need to go back outside to the cabins soon to be sure they were still warm, before it got any darker outside. I offered again to help with him telling me to stay inside where he knew I would be safe, and warm.

He put his arm around me as I leaned my head on his shoulder I drifted asleep again. Aunt Sandy nudged my foot some time later asking me if I was getting hungry. I looked at the clock, and it was almost six o'clock. Tommy had already gotten up, dressed for the cold weather and ready to go back outside to check on the cabins again. It was pitch black outside making it difficult for Tommy to see just a few feet in front of him.

Aunt Sandy handed Tommy a flashlight, and a small walkie talkie as he had headed out the door. Both Aunt Sandy and I watched him go from one cabin to another as we had done earlier that day. If he gave us a thumbs up after coming out of the cabins we couldn't tell because it was so dark, and the snow blowing as hard as ever.

We lost track of him for a short time, and poor Aunt Sandy was worried something bad had happened to him. That was when we heard the back door open with him stepping inside. He looked like a snow monster with all the snow clinging to him, and he was shaking like a leaf. He said all the cabins were working great as he quickly took off his coat, and boots.

I helped him to the couch covering him with the blanket while Aunt Sandy poured him a cup of hot coco she had made. His hands were blue, and hurt to move. I placed them in between my hands rubbing them with mine. He didn't resist it either. I was worried about frost bite, but it didn't look like they were that bad. He had icicles dangling from his hair and eyebrows that quickly melted after a few minutes.

Once he got warmed up he was happy to eat a hot meal. Most of it was leftovers from last nights dinner, but it was warm, and tasted even better than last night. We were so concerned about Tommy, and without a doubt, I was actually worried.

We decided to stay the night downstairs by the fire so we'd stay warm. Aunt Sandy pulled the sofa bed open for her and I to sleep on. Tommy took the love seat for himself to curl up on, because he definitely couldn't stretch out on that as tall as he was. I heard him during the night add logs onto the fire to keep us warm. I swore I also heard him whisper into my ear a soft goodnight with a gentle kiss my forehead, before he went back to the love seat himself. I didn't mind it one bit either. I was happy with my life now, and nothing was going to change how I feel.

ℒIARS

After the horrible snow storm let up, our power was restored. Tommy was outside plowing the driveway for us, and several of our neighbors. Aunt Sandy had made daily phone calls to the neighbors checking on them during the storm to see if they were okay, or needed anything. Everyone seemed to be doing great because they were prepared for this storm. Most people have extra items on hand during the winter just in case something like this happens. Many knew what might happen just from experience and warned others to do the same.

Tommy had a little business of his own, by plowing driveways clear of snow whenever needed. He had a long list of people requesting his service already. He usually didn't get busy until after Christmas, but this storm making its presence known like it had, snowed everyone in.

Tommy had taken a thermos full of hot coffee, and a

few sandwiches, with him to eat, when he got the chance between jobs. The wind was still blowing hard making it difficult to see where the driveways were at times, and drifts were forming as fast as they were plowed through. It was late night before he pulled back into the driveway exhausted, only to get up the next morning for a repeat of the same.

I helped Tommy the best I could by taking the calls, and setting up times when they could expect him to be at their houses. Tommy and I were able to communicate with that set of walkie talkies so he could get to the many houses needed without having to drive back to the house each time. As soon as he finished one driveway, he would get right to the next one. I would phone the people to let them know he was on his way.

Everyone was grateful for him to be able to plow their driveway out on such a short notice. I couldn't imagine where anyone would go in this weather, but I'm sure there were a few that had to. Many just wanted the comfort knowing if they had to get out for some reason, they could.

Aunt Sandy and I waited for him, with a hot meal ready when he returned home, before he took a hot shower, and hitting the sack. He was glad when the phone calls started to be less and less. Most people only needed their driveways plowed five maybe six times during the winter. Tommy never had to advertise his services because word of mouth did it all for him. He did very well doing this service, and it gave him additional money for himself.

Christmas had been wonderful this year. Everyone liked the gifts from me, and I did as well myself. The necklace was beautiful that Tommy got me. A pearl in the center with two diamonds on each side. He put it on me right away, and I gave him a hug. Also there was a gift certificate with a weekend reservation at the ski lodge for a weekend for me and three girlfriends. No one signed it, and no one claimed it was from them either. I thought it would make a perfect girls weekend skiing. I looked forward to skiing again, too.

Strangely enough, Tommy received one just like mine, and for the same weekend. I knew then it had to have been from Aunt Sandy, but she insisted it was not her leaving me wondering who then. She told me it had to have been from Santa Claus, and she winked after stating that, giving it away. I was going to have fun, and finally get back on skis that I missed doing every winter in New York. New York had several ski slopes to go to, but Phillip didn't like skiing, and he definitely didn't like the idea of me going either. Probably because he knew I would enjoy myself, and he couldn't handle that!

After our delicious dinner, we watched a movie nibbling on the many desserts previously prepared. I was stuffed to the gills when I decided it was time for me to go to bed. It was a wonderful Christmas, and I was glad to be home with my loved ones.

The towns New Years Eve party wasn't canceled after all. Many didn't think it would be held because of that snowstorm, but by then everything was open, and businesses were busy once again. I was looking forward to going to the party. Aunt Sandy wore her usual gown of gold sequins on top of a cream knit. It was always stunning on her. I chose to wear a deep purple gown embellished with silver strands of threads. My pearl necklace from Tommy was perfect around my neck. When I came down the stairs to leave, Tommy let out a whistle making me blush for the first time in ages.

Tommy escorted both of us to the party. He looked so handsome all in black wearing the cologne I got him for Christmas. People greeted us immediately as we walked through the community center door adorning us with the traditional party hats for the festivities. Tommy placed a crown on my head telling me a princess should never be without her crown. I had to admit, I surely looked beautiful, and felt like a princess should. Tommy looked distinguished in his top hat loaded with glitter getting it on everything.

The evening was going great in every way. I danced with several men, and even Tommy's buddies, throughout the night. The food was delicious with the appetizers amazing. It felt wonderful being around all these people. The evening was going by so fast. Many people were in small groups talking about the snowstorm we had, and how a few were worried it wasn't going to be the last. Aunt Sandy stopped the nonsense talk telling them to enjoy the night, forget about the weather. We have no control over Mother Nature, but we do have a say on enjoying ourselves.

Everything was going great until the count down to the new year. Tommy found me in the crowd, and counted the last ten seconds down with me. When he kissed me it sent shock waves through me like they had before, but more intense this time. I didn't think I had anymore feelings towards him, but everything was coming back to me that involved him. I still loved him more than what I wanted to ever admit.

Aunt Sandy was riding home with Fred and Marie, so Tommy and I left in his car at the same time. Once we got in the driveway I lost it. I turned to him asking how he could kiss me like he did when he couldn't bother to answer any of my letters when I went away to college. He looked at me with a confused look on his face. He tried telling me he did write to me, and he had the audacity to say he never received any letters from me. I was wild with anger by then. I wrote to him every single day for two years without ever hearing back from him. I dropped it down to once a week to once a month the following year. I just couldn't understand why he could sit next to me, and lie as he was. When he didn't show up for my graduation with Aunt Sandy, I knew we were over then, and we were over because he obviously didn't care.

I called him so many names, beside the nicest one of him being a liar. Everything I had bottled up over the years just spewed out of my mouth in anger, and for the life of me, I couldn't stop. It could have been the liquid courage I felt at the moment from drinking several glasses of champagne at the party, but that wasn't an excuse I could blame it on. I opened the door to get out, and he shouted at me that I was the liar. He had never received a single letter from me ever, and he had wrote many many letters. Told me I needed to quit accusing him of not caring, and the name calling, when I was just that myself. The last thing he said was that I needed to quit acting like a mean persnickety bitch, as I slammed the car door shut stomping into the house.

I wasn't going to listen to him lie to me. I had had more than my share of men lying to me. No wonder they couldn't be trusted, they only knew how to lie. All those letters I wrote, and he never received a single one. Who did he think he was? I wasn't going to fall for that from him, or anyone else. He had balls of brass to say what he did. If it came down to it, I would leave, and find a job somewhere else, away from here. I didn't need him, his lies, or his presence near me. I was hurt before, and never thought I would be able to trust another man again, and this all proved me right.

I went to my room slamming my door shut as hard as I could. Then I reopened it, and slammed it again, even harder. I changed out of my gown, threw that crown in the waste can, took the make up off my face scrubbing it as hard as I could, and went to bed still crying. I want to sleep hoping it was all a nightmare, already knowing it wasn't.

So Tommy thought I was the one lying, and called me a mean persnickety bitch. What nerve he had to say that when he was the liar, not me. I hadn't lied, and he tried throwing the accusation on me. What a jerk!

I heard Tommy open his door, and quietly close it. The bathroom light switched on, and he gently knocked on my side of the pocket door. I didn't answer him. I didn't want to talk anymore tonight, or listen to anymore of his lies. I wanted him to know how he hurt me, and broke my heart. He finally left, and I heard him turn his light off. I was not going to be a part of his joke any longer.

The next morning when I woke up I was so tired yet. I had a bad night trying to sleep thinking of everything that had happened. I cried so much throughout the night. My eyes were still red and puffy, when I looked in the mirror. I grabbed my robe making my way downstairs for a cup of coffee. The house was quiet. Unusually quiet. Aunt Sandy looked up over her cup of coffee she was sipping at the table. She had a concerned look on her face when I sat down at the table with my coffee, and I burst into tears again.

She said Tommy had already told her his side of the events last night, and she wanted to hear mine. I finished by asking her if she remembered Tommy getting letters from me while I was gone. She had remembered, and said she put them in Thomas's mail slot so he could give it to Tommy each time. I asked her over and over why Tommy would call me a liar, when he was the one who never wrote back. She placed her warm hands over mine telling me he did write to me. He put it in the outgoing mail all the time, so why I didn't receive them was baffling to her.

Nothing was making sense at all. I was going crazy, and just didn't realize it until now. I finished my coffee with Aunt Sandy, making my way back to bed. I couldn't face life anymore. Everything was not adding up at all. I fell asleep with my pillow still damp from the tears I shed. I could handle sleep, I was safe then, and had nothing in my way to make me sad when I was asleep.

I heard noise coming from the kitchen now and then, before I drifted back to sleep. I didn't want to know who was talking, or what they were talking about. I wanted to stay asleep where I was numb to anything else happening.

I went downstairs only when I knew Aunt Sandy and Tommy were asleep, to get myself something to eat. I saw several notes written to me on the table, but ignored them. I was sure they were nothing but more lies, and I didn't need to hear anymore lies. I was beginning to think maybe even Aunt Sandy had lied to me as well, she heard Tommy's side before she heard mine. I was a loser when it came to men, and they were all laughing at me behind my back.

I fell back asleep, and when I woke up the next morning Aunt Sandy told me Barb was here to visit me. I didn't want any visitors, and tried to get out of it, but Barb insisted on seeing me. I finally agreed going downstairs, but knew the minute she brings up Tommy's name, I would retreat to my bedroom immediately.

Barb had concern written on her face for me, as we sat there making short talk. I thought she'd leave after a few minutes, but she didn't. She stayed, and after an hour, I started feeling a little better. She brought up the ski trip wondering if it was still on. I wasn't sure I should go, and thought maybe I'd give her the gift certificate she could use with the other girls.

Barb wouldn't hear of it. They were all looking forward to it, and it wouldn't be fun without me. I didn't want to ruin their weekend, but she thought it would do us all good to get away. We all were stressed during the holidays, the snowstorm, and depressed that the holidays were already over, so it was a good weekend to look forward to.

I agreed to go, not expecting to have any fun, or them have any fun with me around. I was so full of self pity, and hate, right now that I couldn't see how I'd have fun. Barb was glad it was still on, and was looking forward to it, emphasizing we'd have fun no matter what. She finally got up to leave, and I sat there enjoying the warmth of the fireplace.

Since I decided to go after all, I needed to find my ski bibs, skis and boots. I have no clue where they could be after all these years, and didn't even know if they'd fit, but I would look for them the next day.

Aunt Sandy was going to be gone with Maria for the day getting things ready for their yearly lady cruise with their friends. They will be gone two weeks enjoying themselves in the warm weather while being pampered daily. They have been doing this for several years now, and I was glad they had that opportunity. They always enjoyed themselves, and being with their friends. Friends were important to her, and she had some very nice ones that enjoyed life the best they could. She always said friends were better than going to therapy. Maybe she needed it more this year with the added baggage I brought home with me.

First thing the next morning I started looking for the box Aunt Sandy had said she put all my ski clothes in, but couldn't remember where she stashed it. I searched the attic in the house, but it wasn't there. All the closets proved empty as well. My next thought was the basement, and after several hours of searching that, it also didn't hold the box she was certain she put everything in.

My last resort was the attic in the garage. Don't know why it would be there, but I gave it a shot after lunch. I bundled up to trek over to the garage to search, with it still colder than heck outside. Glad the garage was heated, and I was able to remove my coat, and gloves once inside.

I don't know how many boxes I opened looking inside without any luck. I was ready to give up, and just go buy new, when I noticed two tubs back in the corner with dust so thick on them, because they hadn't been opened in a long long time. My stuff had to be in there. That made perfect sense to me to be there with all the layers of dust on it. It has been many years since I needed any ski apparel.

I climbed over the rafters towards the tubs thinking I found my stuff at last. I opened the first tub, and couldn't believe what I had stumbled on. It wasn't my clothes at all, but as I sat back on my knees my heart started beating fast, and hard. My mouth went completely dry as I just gawked into the tub. I quickly took the lid off the second tub to find the same things in that as well. I was completely shocked.

𝒫ROOF

There before me in those tubs, were all these letters. On top of the pile was a letter to each of us, Tommy, Aunt Sandy, and to me from Uncle Thomas. I took out the letters written to us, as I slowly ran my fingers through the tub lifting the other letters. Letters I had written to Tommy, which they were never opened. My mind wasn't able to comprehend the whole thing at all, and about ready to explode with this find.

I quickly reached for the other tub which held more letters yet. I lifted them noticing several were written to me. What the hell was going on? I snatched the letters to show Tommy and Aunt Sandy, rushing down the attic stairs. I needed to show Tommy that I had send him letters, he just didn't open them for whatever reason. I caught him at his own deceitful game of lies, and was more than happy to expose him, finding the letters with his little secret out. I replaced the lids on the dusty tubs and as heavy as they were, I finally got them down the stairs and inside the house.

I had dragged both the tubs into the house, up the stairs dumping the tubs out onto Tommy's bedroom floor letting them scatter all over the floor where he couldn't help but see them when he went to his room later. Just to let him know that I found them, catching him in his lies. Even though he never opened them, he had received them, unlike what he had told me. I wanted him to feel the pain I went through, and feel it badly.

I was inside the house so quick I hadn't noticed that I forgot to put my coat or gloves back on. I was so furious by now. I had thought after thought running through my head on his accusations of me not writing, calling me a liar. Proof right in front of me now, to win this battle of lies.

Aunt Sandy walked in shortly after me, and was glad to see me up. Her smile faded quickly when she saw me not smiling back. I gave her a look of pure disgust. I didn't want to spoil her day right now, but I was going to expose my discovery at dinner to both of them at the same time, and let them know how hurtful it has been to know I have been living in a house where people felt they had to lie to me.

I was going to let them both know that I would be leaving here as soon as I found another job somewhere else, and they could stay there in their own bubble without making me miserable any longer. I have been hurt for the last time, and I wasn't going to stick around any longer to let it happen again.

Supper went just fine. Tommy sat across from me never lifting his eyes towards me what-so-ever. Aunt Sandy was her pleasant self trying to make small talk without any success. I just glared at the both of them throughout dinner whenever I looked up.

Almost done with dinner knowing I had to make my move then, and there. I had thought it over and over in my head during the afternoon, while holed up in my room seething with their lies. My thoughts were grinding in my heart and head, on how wrong they had been towards me, and the deceit which fell upon me once again, was all I could take to not lose it completely.

I stood up, and proudly plopped their letters from Uncle Thomas in front of them as I went into my well rehearsed speech on how I felt betrayed, and that they had lied to me for the last time. I could no longer live in a house with liars and secrets, this house seemed to hold.

Tommy was just staring at me, and I knew he thought I was full blown crazy by now, but I wouldn't let up on what I had to say, or give him the chance to open his mouth for another lie to spill out. After all, he had been caught now, and I was exposing all their lies and giving it everything I had, to let him knew what a low life he was, besides being a liar, that he probably didn't think anyone would ever find out. But I did, and I wasn't going to let the matter drop.

I spun around to Aunt Sandy who sat there just staring at me as I told her how I felt, and how disappointed I was with her, and her lies as well. She didn't need to lie to me, all she had to tell me was the truth, and I wouldn't have bothered her any longer. I had thought the world of her, and extremely grateful she had taken me in as she had, caring for me when my mother had passed, but now wondered if she really wanted me back when I left New York, and not have any other place to go to. I must have screwed up the plans for her retirement by popping back into the picture with all the problems I had brought with me.

I quickly told them they were both full of hate, and I had lost the respect I had for them, before I quickly retreated to my room where I felt safe. I laid on the bed crying for hours. Not for what I had said to them, but for how I felt they had toyed with my heart, and with my life. I had been such a fool here as much as I had been in New York.

I heard Tommy go into his bedroom later that night, and heard him grunt in disgust about the mess I had made with the pile of letters scattered on his floor. I heard the tubs slide across the floor knowing he was picking them up, and putting them back in the tubs. I was expecting him to come in at any moment to yell at me for making that mess, but he didn't. I heard him climb in bed and switch off his light. Well, that was no fun.

During the night I woke up to what sounded like a muffling sound which was coming from Tommy's room. I quietly got out of bed, and tip toed to the door to listen, to see what was going on, and it sounded like he was crying. I smiled as I went back to bed thinking that now he knows what its like to have his heart manipulated with.

My heart was so broken now. I didn't think it could or would, ever be the same as it was before with Tommy or Aunt Sandy. They had betrayed me. I fell asleep shortly after my head hit the pillow, and was glad to be asleep where pain and hurt couldn't touch me.

Once light hit my windows, I woke up immediately opening my laptop searching on the internet looking for jobs and apartments in other towns. I had money saved from my New York misadventure yet, and that would be plenty to hold me over for a several months. There was absolutely nothing in the paper on either prospect that met my idea of a good choice. Guess it wasn't a good time of the year to be job searching which was another a disappointment for me. I knew I wouldn't give up searching though.

I listened for Aunt Sandy and Tommy to pull out of the driveway, before I ventured downstairs to get breakfast. I didn't want to see them face to face, or have anything else to do with them any longer. It was odd eating alone in the kitchen, but it was something I was going to have to get use to once I leave here.

I had felt so safe and comfortable here, in what I thought was my home, and it was all a rouse to them. I was so blind to it once again, as I had been with Phillip. I would never let that happen to me again, even though I had said that after leaving New York. I bet they had a good laugh over me and my problems, once I poured my heart out to them, but I would get the last laugh once I leave. This time it would be for good though.

I dodged them for the next two days. Even though I didn't have any luck with a job search, I didn't give up. My midnight trips to the kitchen was becoming easier to do, and even though I remained quiet, I knew Aunt Sandy had heard me. Heard me, but never came out to see me. I got the hint loud and clear, and was fine with that. I was letting her suffer as I have been for so long.

The next morning after Tommy and Aunt Sandy had left, I went downstairs as usual, but this time Maria was there sitting at the kitchen table. I stopped in my tracks at the doorway not knowing if I should turn around, and retreat back to my bedroom, or continue getting myself some breakfast, then retreat.

I chose the later, and when Maria looked up at me from reading the paper, I knew she already knew what had happened. She asked me to sit down with her, as she poured me a cup of coffee. She watched me cautiously saying she had heard what happened a few days ago. I didn't want to be there with her if she was mad at me too, but she insisted she wasn't mad or upset, but was actually glad to see me.

She took my hands in hers telling me she has had love for me ever since she came to work for Aunt Sandy, and understood how I was feeling now. I didn't answer her because I didn't feel I needed to. She then asked if I had read the letter to me from Uncle Thomas, which I told her I hadn't. She asked just one favor of me when I went back upstairs, and that was to sit down to read the letter he wrote, before making any other decisions with my life. It was important to her for me to read it, as if she knew what was in it, and I begrudgingly agreed. She smiled as she came around the table to give me a hug.

We ate breakfast together before I went back to my room to start another job search. I scrolled down through many job openings, but nothing listed in my field. I slammed the laptop close, and went back to sleep.

When I woke up, it was dark outside and in the house. I was wondering where everyone was. No one was home yet, and it wasn't like them.

I saw the letter sitting my the top of my dresser from Uncle Thomas. It was as if there was a beacon of light shinning down upon it for some odd reason to get my attention, so decided to read it as I had promised Maria I would.

I started out with the feeling of a "so what attitude" as it turned into a letter that angered me, caused my heart to beat hard and fast, and then into tears, and my hands trembling out of control.

Thomas had written the letter a few months before he died explaining so many things. I shook my head in disbelief as I read sentence after sentence. Uncle Thomas explained his actions, but knew a few years later he had made the biggest mistake ever, and was actually seeking forgiveness now.

Uncle Thomas explained he wanted Tommy to make something better of his life. Better than his own life had been, and definitely better than the path Tommy's parents had chose. He explained he didn't think Tommy could do it with me around, or in his thoughts all the time, so he decided the only way he could do it was not give him that link connecting us that we had for each other to continue.

After Tommy completed college passing the bar exam, he realized how wrong he had been to interfere with our lives. Then it was too late, because I had moved on with my life in New York, and was engaged to marry. He was at a loss of what to do by then, other than to write the letters asking for our forgiveness.

Uncle Thomas assured me Tommy was still very much in love with me, and if I ever have the chance to read this letter, to understand he was thinking with his heart, and not with his head. Uncle Thomas needed me to forgive him for everything he had done, and wished me the best in my life.

I was shocked at the revelations I had just learned. Tommy wasn't at fault for not answering my letters, Uncle Thomas was. He had taken the letters from the out going pile on Aunt Sandy's desk that Tommy wrote, and never told Tommy I wrote to him. Uncle Thomas kept them all from Tommy, as well as the ones Tommy wrote to me. Both Tommy and I had been played, but I had been played the bigger fool.

All the things I had said to Tommy and to Aunt Sandy, were racing through my mind now. I didn't believe either one of them, and talked so harshly at them when they weren't at fault what-so-ever. All I could do is hold my shaky hand over my mouth, and was barely able to breath.

I was so wrong not to believe them, and now it looks like I was going to pay the price for all the hurtful things I said, and thought. I had turned my back on the ones who loved me the most with my spiteful words, hate, and actions. I didn't deserve them, or their love. I sat on the edge of my bed thinking over and over how I was to ever ask for their forgiveness, but I knew I had to try. I wouldn't be able to live with myself if I didn't.

I knew I had to do it right away. After stumbling down the stairs in the dark, I made it to Aunt Sandy's bedroom door where I tapped softly on the door waiting for her to answer, to allow me to enter. It wasn't long before I heard her tell me to come in. She sat up in bed as I rushed to her side.

My eyes were full of tears that made their way down my cheeks. I shook my head, holding out in front of me, Uncle Thomas's letter. Aunt Sandy patted a spot on her bed for me to sit on, and I crumbed into her arms where I continued to cry. She patted my back, as she had when I was a little girl when my mom had died. She whispered everything was going to be alright now. She loved me unconditionally, and was so sorry what had happened.

I repeatedly told her how sorry I was for everything I had said to her, and for not believing her when she wasn't even aware of what happened either. I added that I would understand if she didn't accept my apology, but I truly apologized for everything because I was so full of hate when I spat out those hurtful things to her.

Aunt Sandy hugged me saying she fully understood what torment I must have been going through. Aunt Sandy said her letter stated almost the same, as I told her what was said in mine. But, she also wanted me to know that she had absolutely no clue what Uncle Thomas had done all those years. It was a guilt he apparently took to the grave with him.

If she had known what deceit he had done to me, her only family, she would have never married him. Aunt Sandy was hurt that he had kept this from her all those years, and live as if everything was alright. She said I didn't need to apologize for it either, but I insisted I did, and she graciously accepted my apology.

We talked a lot about the whole situation, and I could hear her voice change several times as I'm sure she was crying, and in the dark, it was hard to see. Before I got up to leave, she told me that Tommy loved me very much, and she hopes I can forgive him as well. I let her know he had nothing to apologize to me about. I was the one who flew off the handle saying all the harsh words to him that I could muster, as I had done to her.

One thing she said was that Tommy was hurting just as much himself with the fact that the man he looked up to and admired so much, had done something this awful to him. We would have to make sure Tommy understood

125

we were all dealt a hard blow this week. None of us were at fault.

I hugged her and kissed her cheek, before leaving knowing where I was headed to next. My heart ached with the thought I hurt the people in my life that meant the most to me, and I wondered if the that hurt would ever go away. I had jumped the gun with my hate that I was determined to hurt them with it.

Tommy wasn't in his room yet, so I laid down on my bed to wait. Once I heard him coming up the stairs my heart started beating rapidly once again. I immediately went to the pocket door on his side of the bathroom, and tapped softly. No answer. I tapped again. Still no answer. I finally spoke up telling him I knew he was in there, and he wasn't asleep that fast. I waited until I heard him walk over to unlatch the door to pull it open.

He looked down at me with a blank look on his face. I could tell he had been out drinking with his friends by the smell of beer on his breath, when he asked me what I wanted in a disgusted tone. My heart sank as I could hear the annoyance in his voice he used talking to me. I asked if he would just hear me out, and he stood there waiting with that annoyance written all over him.

My tears were on the edge of falling as I profusely told him how sorry I was for everything I had said and accused him of, and how I wish I could take everything back everything that flew out of my big mouth the other day. I was so wrong not to believe him, and did everything to destroy our friendship. I explained I had just read his grandfather's letter earlier, and knew then Tommy had told the truth all along. I had told the truth all along myself. I asked for his forgiveness telling him to take his time to think about it, if he'd like. I hoped it would be the decision I wanted to hear, but who knows at this point. He stood there just staring at me running his hand through his hair. I had expected him to just shut the door in my face, so I stepped aside to let him, and slowly turned away to walk back into my room.

Tommy grabbed my arm, swinging me around to face him, saying he didn't need any time to decide on forgiving me. We had both been deceived by his grandfather, and as he pulled me towards him, he cupped the side of my face, bringing his mouth down to mine to kiss me. My heart was beating hard, but it was of happiness now. Tommy told me he accepted my apology even though I didn't have to apologize.

I assured him I did, for all the rotten things, and nasty name calling I had said to him. He interrupted me, reminding me about his name calling to me as well. I told him he wouldn't have done it if I hadn't said those horrendous things to him first, so he had nothing to apologize about. He kissed me again. When he released me, he said he had never stopped loving me all these years.

I leaned into him, and started crying. I told him I felt like I was losing my mind with everything that has happened in my life. Tommy held me tightly in his arms saying he wouldn't let that ever happen again to me. He wanted to help me mend my broken heart, and help pick up the shattered pieces to my life, making me the Lexi he knew before, if I would only let him.

All I could do was nod my head yes. That was all we needed that night agreeing we would talk more in the morning. Tommy walked me back to my bed, and when I got in, he covered me up planting a kiss on my forehead, before going back to his room. He left the bathroom doors open between us, which made me smile. I felt it was symbolic of our lives being open to each other once again.

I was so tired I fell asleep immediately. Tired, but knowing I had my family willing to forgive me made all the difference.

A New Beginning

I woke up bright and early the next morning, to the kitchen noise drifting up to my room, with the aromas of fresh brewed coffee, bacon frying, and homemade bread from the kitchen. Aunt Sandy was busy making breakfast for us as she was jubilantly humming to herself. It was good to see her cheerful, and hear her humming one of her favorite hymns. I watched her for a few minutes from the doorway before I entered in her kitchen.

She turned smiling at me, and I gave her a hug like I had all the years before with her. She asked if everything was okay between me and Tommy now. For the first time in a long time, a smile crept across my face at the mention of his name, and I nodded an affirmative yes. I could tell she was happy with that answer, too.

Shortly, as the toast popped up, Tommy walked in, still wearing his pajama bottoms, and his hair a disheveled mess with red bloodshot eyes. None the less, he was still a good sight to see. He walked over giving Aunt Sandy a hug, and then to me. He hadn't done that since before I left for college.

We sat down, and after Aunt Sandy said grace, we ate as if we hadn't eaten a thing all week. After breakfast was done, and dishes put in the dishwasher, Aunt Sandy asked for Tommy and me to stay a few minutes. She had something she felt we needed to talk about right away. I could tell it was serious from the tone of her voice.

We all sat back down at the table as she began by telling us how happy she was to see us both in the same room together again, and on friendly terms. She started out by telling us how much we meant to her, and what had happened, was horrible to all three of us, not just to one. Something that didn't need to happen, shouldn't have happened, but did happen, and we needed to all work together to mend our little family. She said she always felt Tommy as part of the family ever since he moved here to live with his grandfather, and that she felt the same then, as she does today.

Tommy spoke next barring his feelings on how sorry he was for what his grandfather had done to hurt us, as he had. He wasn't sure how he felt about him now, and that was when Aunt Sandy interrupted saying the situation in a nut shell, stating that his grandfather reacted with his heart, and definitely not with his head. I sat there thinking about that statement, realizing that was what Uncle Thomas had done exactly to us, to all three of us. He only wanted what was best for Tommy, but he just didn't go about it the right way. It was still a hard pill to swallow when we think about all the years wasted, when we could have been so happy together.

By the time we all had our say about the mess, we were

all in tears, and decided to make our family go on with open honesty, and the love for each other as we had before the whole mess started, and was discovered. We'd have to help each other along the way, as we each needed mending differently in one aspect, or another. We agreed that was the best for all of us, and after several hugs, we smiled making it our first day, of our new chapter in our lives together.

Aunt Sandy had another committee to go to concerning her cruise, and excused herself leaving Tommy and me, at the table still talking. Tommy looked over at me smiling as he reached for my hands, holding them as he spoke. He wanted me to know that he meant what he said last night, every word of it, and he would do everything in his power to help me get back to the person he knew I was. I squeezed his hands thanking him. I knew he meant every word he had said, and I was more than happy now.

He had one thing that was puzzling him though. Where and how did I find those totes filled with the letters. I chuckled saying that they were not what I was looking for, by any means. I had been looking for my ski boots, skis, and ski bibs for the upcoming weekend at the ski resort. I had searched the attic, basement, and closets in the house coming up empty handed, thinking the only other place to look, was in the attic above the garage. That was where I found the letters hidden way back in the corner by themselves. Then I went crazy mad and well, he knew the rest of the story.

He shook his head asking if I ever found my ski equipment. I shook my head no.

That was when he got up telling me to get ready, we were going into town to get some new skis, boots, and bibs, because we were still going on that ski trip together with our friends, and he was looking forward to it now more than anything else.

I dashed upstairs getting ready in record time, but still not as fast as Tommy. How did he always beat me dressing, I never could understand.

We ended up having to drive to Saginaw to get what we needed. Tommy needed them as well, so we made a great day of shopping together. We talked nonstop driving there holding hands through the stores as if we were back to our teenage years again. I have to admit, it felt wonderful, too. Tommy always said my hands were so tiny that they fit in his as if they were made to be there all along

After our purchases were made, which were more expensive than I expected they would be, we went to a little café for a late lunch, and relaxed before trekking back home. We were exhausted by the time we got home, but still had energy enough to watch a movie after dinner that night.

Aunt Sandy had been at her red hat meeting most of the day discussing their plans while they were on the cruise. They go every year for ten days on a cruise. This year it was to Mexico, with a few extra days before and after, that they attend a play, opera, or whatever they find happening during their spare time. I was glad she had such a nice group of ladies to have fun with. They were all very close, and started going on these cruises many years ago. Maria was also in this group, and would be gone as well during that time.

Aunt Sandy was excited about going, sharing all the plans they were making with me. It sounded like she was going to have a wonderful time, and she deserved it. Especially this past year. It had been a rough one for her, too.

Aunt Sandy decided to go to bed early that night, while

Tommy and I finished the movie before we went upstairs ourselves. Tommy had checked all the door locks as I switched off the lights. He walked me to my door kissing me the sweetest kiss to say good night. I made sure that kiss lingered longer than last night's kiss, as I could feel my body reacting to him in every way. He broke away, and walked quickly to his room smiling from ear to ear.

My heart was beating uncontrollably, and I knew he was getting to me. I had the same feelings for him now, if not more, than when I left for college. Aunt Sandy had always said, you don't have to travel far away for love, when sometimes it's found in your own backyard. At that time I knew she was referring to Uncle Thomas, but it could also been said for me.

I laid in bed that night thinking of everything that has happened the past several months. I always believed that things happen to you for a reason, and maybe finding Phillip with Heather was a way of telling me I needed to get away from Phillip, to move back home, to where there was someone who loved me, who really loved me.

I know I was in love with Tommy again, otherwise I wouldn't accept his passionate kisses as I do, or enjoy being with him as much as I am. Whenever I see him, my whole body would get the tingling sensation. Was I happy with that, was I ready to begin, or in this case rekindle, the love with another man, yet the same man? I am, and I think moving on with Tommy at my side will do me good to becoming whole once again.

Sleep isn't a way to escape my unhappiness anymore. I would wake up knowing I had a good day ahead of me, and actually looked forward to enjoying life itself. Sleeping was bringing me good dreams more and more often now.

I spoke with Aunt Sandy about how I was feeling about everything, and if she thought it was too soon to start being with Tommy, as a couple again. She said to follow my heart, and she would support any decision I make. She didn't think half a year was too short to wait after my ordeal with Phillip. After all, Phillip didn't even wait for our relationship to be over before he moved on with Heather. We both knew Tommy was still in love with me, and how he told Aunt Sandy he wished he could get me to open my eyes to him again. What we had was special, very special, and I knew it could only get better with time.

Tommy left sweet little things around the house for me. Sayings he found that reminded him of me, and short sweet poems he wrote himself. I saved all of them in my little box full of memories. I placed them in it before getting into bed. They were special things, and it showed me I was on his mind all the time. The way couples should be.

I left him a small jar filled with pennies one day. I didn't know my little piece of paper had fallen off that read, "A penny for your thoughts", and he was puzzled by it. I found the paper on the floor giving it to him right away. He smiled stating I needed a larger jar for all the thoughts he had concerning me.

Our kisses started to get more intense when we said our good-nights. I wanted more than a good night kiss from him. Last night when he kissed me good night he told me he didn't know how much longer he could go on just kissing me, when he really wanted me completely.

I told him one of these nights, I wasn't going to walk into my room alone either. He smiled as I closed my door. My heart and feelings were racing wildly now, and I rushed to the bathroom doors just as he was closing his door telling him that it was one of those nights already.

Tommy came over swooping me into his arms kissing me long and hard, as he guided me to my bed. He whispered into my ear if I was sure I wanted what was about to happen, and I nodded yes.

He slowly removed my clothes piece by piece, dropping them to the floor as I tugged his shirt off exposing that chest containing a six pack of muscles.

I reached down to unbuckle his jeans, but they were already sliding down his long legs being kicked off to the side. Tommy ever so gently lowed me to my bed where we made the most passionate love. He was all I needed, and all I wanted.

We crawled under the covers afterwards, and I laid my head across his chest. He was so warm as he caressed my arm so gently as I fell asleep. I was content and very happy for the first time in a long time.

I woke up earlier than normal playing the night through my head several times. I didn't want to compare Tommy to Phillip, but I can assure you, Phillip could have taken some lessons from Tommy on making love from the way we did last night. My goodness, I didn't remember Tommy's manly part the way it is now. I'm not complaining by any means, it was all good in my book. All very good!

Tommy stirred waking up, running his hands over my body ever so gently which caused my body to start react sensuously, and before I could think anymore, we made love once again. I can't explain how wonderful it felt, but I knew Tommy and I were meant to be together, and I now felt comfortable with how things were turning out.

We laid on the bed afterwards when he whispered in my ear that he loved me. I know I'm in love with him as well, and yet, I had the hesitation in telling him so. I had said those three words so often and after my ordeal with Phillip, it seemed as if those words had been cheapened now. I will tell Tommy that I do love him in time, but until then, he'll have to understand why. He had me, hook, line, and sinker. Funny how that phrase can mean different things when used in other ways. This was the hook, line, and sinker I wanted.

We could smell the bacon frying, and coffee being brewed, so we got up. I rushed to the shower lathering my body with shower gel when Tommy climbed in behind me. He ran his hands over my body distributing the soap to all parts known to mankind. I turned to lather him up when we heard Aunt Sandy knock on my bedroom door as she called to rise and shine, breakfast was ready. It put an immediate halt on our shower together rather quickly, as we rinsed off, got out, and dressed.

Later that day Tommy and I packed our bags for the weekend. We had our skis and poles setting by door the for our ski trip. Betty and Mike were going to ride up with us when we leave in the morning. Aunt Sandy baked several different things for us to take, and wanted to be sure we'd have the room for them. There's always room for her bake goods.

I was looking forward to this ski trip ever since I read Uncle Thomas's letter, and had apologized to Tommy and Aunt Sandy profusely. It was amazing how I felt last week at this time about them, and how everything came around to where we are, to how I feel today. I am finally able to move past the hatred I felt towards Phillip too, and be happy. And I was happy. I had friends I enjoyed being around, my aunt with me, and especially with Tommy. I can't imagine anything being better.

Tommy made sure all the cabins would be fine while we're gone, while Aunt Sandy and I had some time to talk alone. She was feeling better about the betrayal of Uncle Thomas, not forgiving him totally yet for his part in the whole ordeal, and looking forward to her trip a few days after we get back from skiing.

She flat out asked me if I was going to be alright now with everything that had happened, and if Tommy and I were together again. I beamed from ear to ear on that topic, telling her I was fine, and yes, Tommy and I were a couple again. She was pleased as she hugged me. I assured her she wouldn't have to worry about me getting pregnant this time around either. We both chuckled over that.

THE INTRUDER

O ur drive to the ski lodge was very pleasant with me sitting next to Tommy. Tommy and I listened to the radio most of the way, when we weren't talking with Betty and Mike. We had all the ski gear and luggage, in the back of Tommy's covered pickup truck, while the others rode together in a separate vehicle, which gave us time to talk about everything under the moon. It was nice, relaxing, and I was happier than I have been in such a long time.

Once we got to the lodge, the guys were busy unpacking the truck, while the rest of us put things in the refrigerator, and into our separate rooms. It made the time go by so fast, and before we knew it we were relaxing in front of the stone fireplace in our cabin. Betty grabbed a bottle of wine for us, while the guys drank their beer. I was amazed at how tired I was, but when I thought back to everything that had happened the past few weeks, it didn't surprise me. I felt so drained, needing this little get away, and I wanted it to be great for all of us.

I looked at the huge window overlooking the mountains, when I thought I saw a face peering in. I did an immediate double take, and it was gone. When I got up to look there wasn't anything there, but I knew I hadn't imagined it. I called Tommy over by me and quietly told him what I saw, or what I thought I saw. Tommy decided he'd go outside to look around to ease my mind. He probably thought I was being paranoid, but with the recent phone calls from Phillip telling me I better be watching my back, maybe I was, but I had every right to be. Tommy doesn't know Phillip the way I do, and how low Phillip would stoop to get what he wants. I was glad when Tommy came back inside and quietly whispered to me that there wasn't anything, or anyone, out there giving me a hug to assure me he understood my concerns. But, I knew what I saw, and no one was going to convince me other wise.

Tommy told me there were footprints in the snow under the window, but they could have been there from before our arrival, or even by us for that matter, because no one even paid attention to anything other than getting everything inside the cabin, and out of the cold weather. That was when I started to get a little concerned. I was afraid Phillip was stalking me, or had someone stocking me for him, and was going to make trouble. But, how would he know our cabin number let alone where and when, I would be here. It just had to have been my imagination running rapid through my brain, and I did have a large glass of wine already. I was tired, and thought I just needed some sleep.

We all decided to call it a night as we headed to our

rooms, around midnight. I felt safe in Tommy's arms as we fell asleep, but not as safe as I would be if I were still at home. Tommy had told Aunt Sandy he would take good care of me when we left the house, knowing Tommy would, but there is always that chance I would be taking. I couldn't believe the time when we finally woke up the next morning. We had wanted to spend as much time on the slopes as possible, and needed to get ready as soon as we came back from breakfast at the small restaurant connected to the lodge.

There, at the restaurant, I glanced at the mirrors on the walls, and again, I saw that face from the night before. The same exact face, and I was wide awake with absolutely no wine to impair my sight. I casually leaned over to Tommy, and quietly told him to look at the mirrors by the waitress. Just as soon as he looked, the man hid his face with a menu, then took off leaving the restaurant as fast as he could. It was funny to watch because once Tommy looked that way, our whole group looked in the direction as well, to see what we were looking at. They didn't see anything unusual, or even know what was going on, but it didn't matter. Our snoopy person was gone, and hopefully gone for good.

We spent the entire morning skiing down the slopes. The chairlift hauled us up to the top of the mountains, allowing us a view that was breath taking. The snow was a perfect powder glistening brightly with the sun shining making the day absolutely gorgeous. We stopped long enough to take a few pictures of us and the others, to remember this day for a long time. Making lasting memories with our best friends.

Once again, I thought I saw that face watching us from the wooded area when I was skiing down hill for my last trip down. I didn't dare take my eyes off the slope to get a better look, but I was sure I had seen that face once again! My mind must be playing tricks on me, because there was no reason for someone to be watching us. No reason!! This time he had a camera around his neck that he held up to his face when I went by. The sunlight must have hit the lens causing a flash, drawing my attention towards it. Maybe it was for the lodge to put pictures in an upcoming brochure, or something, but I was going to ask at the front desk before we went to our cabin for the night.

I didn't let it stop me from enjoying my time with Tommy, and our friends. Once we got back to the lodge, I excused myself for a few minutes. I rushed to the front desk to ask if they had hired someone to take pictures of the guest skiing for advertisement or something. They hadn't, and I just knew immediately, it had something to do with Phillip for sure.

I decided not to say anything to anyone else about my suspicion, and I wasn't going to let what I thought might be my imagination running wild to ruin our weekend. We stopped in at the bar ordering a few drinks before heading back to our cabin. Once we were back at the cabin, I could immediately tell someone had been in there going through my stuff. Things I had placed in a certain way had been moved some, not much, but I still knew. And I didn't like it one bit. I was still under Phillip's mind control, and until he stops his antics, I will never feel safe anywhere.

All at once I heard the front door being jerked opened with Tommy running outside yelling at a man. We all ran to see what the commotion was about. Tommy had grabbed the man's camera from him, taking out the memory stick before he thrust the camera back at the man, telling him he'd better leave us alone, and rattled off some legal mumble jumble stuff to him that I had no clue what it meant. That man probably didn't know either, but it was good enough to sound important, and he'd better stay away.

I was shaking by the time the man left, after giving me an evil glare with his eyes. Once we were inside we pulled all the drapes closed tight as Tommy explained he thought he had seen him peering in our windows one other time, but caught him this time in the act of snapping photos. He was definitely up to no good. I was glad Tommy had caught him, and now I knew for sure it wasn't my imagination any longer.

Everyone was puzzled by Tommy's reaction, but I knew, and I thought it was time they knew as well. We sat down explaining to them what was happening with me, who I was, yes, the one who broke Tommy's heart years ago, and a lot about Phillip, and how he has threatened me. How Phillip used me for his gain at the bank he owned, and where I was working for five years. How hard I had worked, and how he gave me absolutely no credit. How I had put my heart and soul into my job, and relationship with him, then seeing him in bed with Heather, a co-worker. He was also cheating his clients on services which he didn't perform, and he is now answering for them in court, with the many lawsuits his clients had filed against him. He also showed up at my Aunt Sandy's resort threaten and assaulted me in front of Tommy, and some other guests, once he located me after I left New York, and again I heard more threats from him the other day over the phone.

As we explained, our friend's eyes were wide as they sat quietly listening to every detail Tommy spoke. It wasn't until we were done that Betty told us she had seen him before in the restaurant, in a booth not far from us, snapping photos of us as well. Others started remembering seeing him around the place as well, but they hadn't thought about anything unusual either. Mostly thought he was there to snap photos of the guests, and then offer us a package deal at the end of our stay to remember our weekend.

I grabbed my laptop from our bedroom to download his memory stick to see exactly what he did have on it. Tommy, and especially me, weren't surprised that every single picture was of us. Me, Tommy, and all our friends. No one else in the photos from the lodge. I was shocked at how many photos were taken of us in the cabin through the window. He had been taking those photos every night we were there. Talk about getting a creepy feeling with chills racing down my spine. How easy it was to have your life spied on, and not even know it was happening.

Betty came over wrapping her arms around me to apologize. I didn't understand for what, until she said for saying all the bad things they had said about Tommy's old love, breaking his heart when we first started out in our friendship. I just smiled telling her I didn't dare tell anyone who I really was, and why I was back in town. I had been humiliated, and deserved what people thought of me, but didn't want everyone knowing everything else that had happened. Everything they had said had been true, so there was no need to apologize. Then, that led into the topic of our letters to each other that were hidden from us all those years by Tommy's grandfather. Guess you can say we were the topic of conversation that night.

We sat around for several hours sipping wine, talking about Phillip, and how we were moving forward from this whole situation. We didn't want the weekend ruined on my account. Everyone agreed they'd keep their eyes open to anything else Phillip might have up his sleeve, and all agreed not to let this ruin it for all of us. They were all there to support us in everything, and if we needed anything, they'd help out. Wow! Talk about us having great supportive friends, we definitely had them!

By the time we went to bed, I was a little bit better at being at ease, but knew things were going to get ugly soon. I tossed and turned all night making it difficult for Tommy to even sleep. I pondered over everything that had happened, and I finally got up going to the kitchen to get some tea, and some of Aunt Sandy's delicious cookies she sent along.

Betty heard me moving around out there, and came out to see if I was okay, as she poured herself a mug of tea, and helping herself to the cookies as well. I did everything in my power to hold the tears back, but they still flooded like a breached dam down my face. I told her I was so sorry to drag them into my mess and on and on about how scared I was about the lawsuit Phillip threatened me with, to the possibility of losing everything I owned, and down to hurting people like I have. Betty assured me they would be there to support me through all of it. We talked for over an hour on everything. I thanked her for listening, and gave her a hug before going back to bed where I fell into a deeply needed sleep.

And sleep I did. I didn't even open my eyes until 11 o'clock the next morning, and the house was so quiet. Everyone had gone to breakfast, except for Tommy. He was busy writing away on his notepad he carried around with him all the time now. Once he saw me awake, he quickly dropped his pen and pad, rushing over to greet me with a kiss, and hugged me ever so gentle. Told me where everyone was then, and that we could join them for lunch at 1:00 if I felt up to it.

I agreed to that, telling Tommy I decided I wasn't going to allow Phillip from stopping me to live my life anymore. I was going to live it, and enjoy it to the max.

The rest of our time there was absolutely wonderful. After lunch we went skating at the nearby pond. I was sitting on the log made into a bench while lacing my skates, when I glanced around to our friends. They were all looking around the area keeping a vigilant lookout for that inquisitive camera man, if he came around again. Tommy and I skated on the pond around and around several times at ease, having a marvelous time. We brought a thermos of hot chocolate to warm our insides with when we stopped for a break. The hot chocolate was the best I had ever taste, and went down smoothly. Maybe because I was trying to be calm, or I was so cold, I don't know, but it hit the spot.

We had a sleigh ride back to the lodge, and as we wrapped ourselves with the heavy blankets, I leaned back into Tommy's arms. It turned out to be a great day even with what had happened the night before. We never saw the "camera man," as we had dubbed him the rest of our time at the ski lodge. The message Tommy gave him must have worked.

After our last dinner at the lodge restaurant we walked back to our cabin, and the guys started a fire to warm it up right away. We had to be out by 11 o'clock in the morning so we didn't worry about packing anything that night. Most of our food was sandwich meat, snacks, and drinks, so we didn't have to pack any of that, just take the extra beer back when we left.

We called it an early night walking into our separate rooms where I fell asleep in Tommy's arms again. I slept like a rock waking the next morning refreshed, and ready to get things packed into the truck to be on our way. I was looking forward to getting home, and seeing Aunt Sandy. Maybe what I really wanted was just to be home where I felt the safest, I don't know. This whole Phillip trial had me frazzled, and on edge all the time wondering when it was going to happen, and what Phillip could do to me.

ALONE WITH TOMMY

A unt Sandy was busy packing her clothes for her cruise with her friends while I was non-stop chattering about the marvelous time we had at the lodge, thanking her again for the weekend get-away. Our talk got really intense when I told her about the camera man that Tommy actually caught in the act of taking pictures of us, through the window of our cabin one night. I had seen him the night before, but no one else had, so I thought I was just losing my mind.

Aunt Sandy stopped packing completely to take in all that information I was telling her. Aunt Sandy thought for several minutes, and with a concerned looked on her face, she asked if I thought Phillip had hired him. I just shook my head yes telling her that I thought of him too, wondering why he would go to such great lengths to spy on me like that. Was there something he had up his sleeve, I wasn't sure,

Joann Buie

but I do know that it gave me such an uneasy feeling for the rest of the weekend.

Aunt Sandy thought maybe she should cancel her cruise with her lady friends to stay home to keep an eye on the house and cabins, in case Phillip was up to something there. I assured her she needed to go on the cruise, and enjoy herself. She deserved it, and besides, I had Tommy there to watch over things, keep me safe, and promised we would look after the resort. I assured her that everything would be okay, with her on her well deserved vacation.

She finally agreed, but she would be checking in on us everyday she could, and we had to promise to keep our eyes and ears open to anything we thought was unusual, and to call the sheriff immediately to have it checked out. She didn't realize, I just wanted to have some alone time with Tommy for a few days, without anyone else around. Maybe a little selfish on my part, but I was going to make this relationship work with every ounce of being in me. I didn't think she'd be in the way, but I wanted my time with him, and only him around. Maybe to see if we were as compatible as we think we are, or maybe to really see if he was the one I could count on in every situation possible. I don't know which, but I was going to find out with Aunt Sandy on her cruise leaving Tommy and me, alone together in the house.

We drove Aunt Sandy to the airport along with Maria, the next morning and once they were off both Tommy and I, looked at each other before bursting out loud laughing like two teenagers ready to party the two weeks away. Once all the ladies were there to board the jet, we left the airport.

Once we got back to the house, I prepared our dinner, watched a movie when everything was cleared from the table, and the dishwasher running. Tommy had a fire lit in the fireplace making it warm. It was really quiet in the house for some reason. A strange quietness that I couldn't put my finger on, but I nestled in Tommy's arms as we watched the movie.

The sky was very dark, as if we were going to get hit with a storm again, even though there wasn't anything in the weather forecast for our area on the news. It didn't matter now, we were home safe, and Aunt Sandy was off to enjoy herself on her cruise. I scanned the outside yard as much as I could see in the dark, doubled checked the doors to be sure they were locked, before turning off the lights before going to bed. Tommy had the same ideas I did, and when he came into my room he told me what he had done. Not only was I having that eerie feeling tonight, but Tommy was also.

Tommy and I had a lengthy conversation before we fell asleep that night about Phillip, and our ski trip. I hadn't been aware of it, but Tommy had been keeping notes on everything that happened, just in case Phillip did take me to court.

That was the first time Tommy finally asked me how I would be able to prove I did the presentation papers completely myself. What encryption had I done, when I talked to him, Aunt Sandy, and Maria, that day? I smiled sitting up in bed telling him how I encrypted them all with a message which was, "These papers were compiled, written, researched, all data collected, and printed solely by me, Alexia Adams, and no one else but me". The letters were in order one at a time in bold print. You would never know they were spelling out a message that no one besides me, and now Tommy knew how, and what I wrote. I told Tommy my old professor in college had told us some ways to cover our butts on things like this, and one night when I went to bed, I remembered it, and made my own testimony of ownership on everything I had worked on.

Tommy was amazed, asking if I was sure I had done it to every project I worked on, and I nodded yes to affirm that. He got the largest smile across his face telling me not to tell anyone about that vital piece of information. It was what he referred to as our "smoking gun". We will blindside Phillip when the time was right with the encryption, and the jury will all be able to see what a snake in the grass Phillip actually was.

It sounded great to me and knew then, I would probably win the case, if Phillip wants to cause a problem with me by saying I stole his work, and that I had been the cause of his business failings.

It was only a matter of a few weeks after Aunt Sandy was home from her cruise that the dreaded letter came in the mail certified to me, from New York City. Aunt Sandy had the look on her face, and I knew immediately the letter in her hand was bad news that was going to tear my life apart again. Phillip hired a top notch law firm to represent him, and he was seeking several hundreds of thousands of dollars, claiming I stole the files on his clients. The files I had put my heart and soul into with the tedious research I had done for the presentation reports that he claimed he did himself. Also for the destruction of the door window at the office, for the several clients he lost after I left, and for defamation of his name, and reputation he highly thought he had. I held the letter in my shaky hands as I reread it over several times. My eyes were filled with tears, and my heart beating rapidly. I could hear my heart thumping in my ears as my chest heaved with shortness of breath. The letter made me sound like I was a horrible person, when all I did was work my butt off for him.

Phillip had all the files available to him. I had the originals with me as I felt they were of my hard work. I had made a list of all the clients I made presentations for with their name, addresses and phone numbers, for some reason. It was only to cover my butt in case something like this would happen, I suppose. It has gone so wrong since he fired me. I'm so glad I had saved all the files, marked them, and how I would now find out how it may help save me, or destroy me, by still having them.

Aunt Sandy tried as hard as she could to console me, but I was not in the mood for it at the moment. I was devastated, hurt, and humiliated all over again. I had hoped everything was in the past, only to have it all brought back up once again. I wondered if it was going to be something that would haunt me the rest of my life. Was I going to have to watch my back every day thinking I would be a target for something more to happen?

I let out the loudest scream my lungs could muster, and threw a few things around in the kitchen. I scared poor Maria half to death and she ran outside in the cold, without her coat on, to locate Tommy to bring him inside.

Tommy came rushing in stopping in his tracks as he saw me on the floor sobbing hysterically clutching the letter still in my fist. Aunt Sandy was next to me dabbing her eyes as she gently rocked me in her arms. Tommy scooted in on the other side of me to comfort me the best he could. Yet, I was so lost, feeling as if my life was completely over, and I didn't care if it was anymore. Everything that involved Phillip was nothing but bad luck, with one thing after another happening to me.

Tommy got me upstairs and into bed, where he remained until I finally fell asleep. No words spoken between us, but having him there was comforting enough, and I did feel safe. Aunt Sandy had called our family doctor who came over quickly to help, and left some pills for me to take to help me cope. Those pills only made me want to sleep, but I slept without any dreams or nightmares, which was probably good.

After several days I was able to sit up in bed, and finally ate some oatmeal Maria had made earlier. Tommy brought it up begging for me to try to eat a few spoons full. It was delicious, and stayed down. I finished every bit of it before falling back to sleep for the rest of the day.

When I got up to use the bathroom, I gasp at the reflection of myself in the mirror. My eyes were sunken in my head with dark circles around them. My hair full of snarls, and my skin was as white as a sheet. I was mortified at what was looking back at me. I then realized this was reality, and not just a nightmare I thought I was having. I needed to wrap my head around this whole situation immediately, and think about how I was going to win the case over Phillip's allegations, to put him in my past..... again! And forever!!

Tommy saw the bathroom light on knowing I was up, and asked if I was up to talking. I knew he must have been concerned about me because I know whenever I opened my eyes, no matter how brief it was, he was there holding my hand.

Tommy and I talked for a long time during the night, and

he told me he had been keeping notes all along of what had been happening, and had started to put my defense together in bits and pieces. He had several questions he needed answers to, to be sure his notes were correct. Tommy said they had to be precise and accurate, without any exaggeration or speculations, so we could have a solid defense. I was amazed at how much he had written down already, and how accurate everything was. He had been writing almost every night since Phillip came to the resort that day making his threats to me. I started to get tired, and we called it quits for the time being, with the promise I would be ready for more questions later in the morning. Tommy picked all the papers up, kissed me, and tucked me back in bed for now.

He started walking back to his room when I asked if he could stay with me. I needed him close to me now, and having his arms around me, I felt protected from anything the world could throw at me. He set the papers down on my dresser, and climbed in next to me under me covers where we both fell asleep.

$\mathcal{P}$REP $\mathcal{W}$ORK

$\mathcal{F}$or the first time in several days I was up, and ready to get started on everything needed for my case. We had a court date in New York in six weeks, and Tommy wanted no time loss at getting it ready. Maria was already there making breakfast for us when I walked into the kitchen. Everyone froze in their spot, and smiled at me. I knew I probably looked a horrible sight, but I was hungry, and I was ready to eat everything I could get my hands on. It felt good to be there, and talking with them. I knew deep in my heart I was going to be okay.

Aunt Sandy assured me no matter the outcome, win or lose, we would make it through Phillip's game, and go from there with our lives. She didn't have any doubt we would win the case in court, but just in case, they were there to support me, and love me no matter what.

Tommy and I worked on the case for five hours before

he called for a break. Tommy could see I was getting tired, and thought I needed to rest more. We went upstairs, and laid down with my head resting on his chest, and his arms around me, where I fell asleep. I was drained, and didn't even realize it.

This went on for several days while we waited for Phillip's papers to be faxed over that were in the discovery stage of the case. We made the reservations for our flight, and hotel stay we would need in New York City. I hope this case wasn't going to be the end of me. I have worked too hard for what I have, and I really didn't want to lose any of it. The stuff Phillip's attorney faxed to Tommy was nothing but junk, and all were just his or Phillip's opinions, with no facts to back anything up, and there was every single project I had done that he claimed he had done, stating I had stole them. There were several photos of me at the resort looking like I was having a great time. I was, until his sneaky photographer made the weekend more of a watch my back because we're coming to get you type of ordeal. Phillip's attorney didn't have many people listed that they planned to call to testify on his behalf, but Tommy explained that wasn't important. It could also be a tactic to throw me off in what I had to say.

Not sure how long the trial would take, we left it open ended for our return with the airlines. Tommy said many times these trials can go for a month, even though the judge has only granted us two weeks on the calendar. We hope mine doesn't take longer than the two weeks, because we have to be back to help Aunt Sandy at the resort. Our opening weekend was approaching quickly, and we really needed to be there.

As Tommy was going over every project he asked me

where I had encrypted them because he couldn't see anything out of the ordinary, and he had looked for several days. Once I showed him every bold letter in order compiled the same message, he looked quickly at each project and smiled....our "smoking gun". He was very pleased that every report had the exact message, and that everyone else had overlooked it. No doubt Phillip, and his high dollar attorneys, had as well. Tommy worked for several hours each day with me to present this case in a professional manner, with only the truth, and solid details. We were going to wait to the very end to produce the encryption leaving Phillip to think all through the trial that he had the case all in his favor.

The six weeks flew by so fast, and before we knew it, we were on our way to New York. Aunt Sandy drove us to the airport, and wished us well as we got out of the car. I could tell she was worried, but did everything she could not to show it.

Once we stepped off the plane, I started to get a very uneasy feeling, and wanting to go back home now. Tommy read the look on my face, and whispered I was going to be fine, and we were going to get through this, one question at a time. He was there to help me do so. If he only understood how much I detested just being in New York City, and knowing I'd have to be in the same room with Phillip. It made my skin crawl just thinking about it.

The judge had told Tommy he couldn't bring up anything about the fraud Phillip had done to his clients bills during this trial. He had already been found guilty of them, and was waiting to hear what his sentence would be. Even though I knew about Phillip doing it, I was never brought into that mess, which is where I thought that problem should stay, with me out of it completely!

Tommy had reserved two adjacent rooms so we could still be together when needed, and it made appearances look professional, which we needed. We didn't want everyone knowing we were a couple and have conflict of interest thrown in our faces. We both ordered room service for the first night meal, which I rolled the cart into Tommy's room where we ate together, once the porter had left. We kept our drapes drawn closed the entire time while in there, and I rumpled the bed sheets and blankets, every morning for maid service to think we were not together. We had the door between our rooms closed as we left to go to the courthouse. It might have been a silly thing to do, but I didn't want anything to go wrong to jeopardize my case. I was probably just being paranoid again, but that's how I felt at the time.

At the courthouse, I didn't think my knees would allow me to climb up the stairs. If Tommy hadn't been by my side, I think I would have turned around, and ran. For the first few hours, a batch of possible jurors were present where the judge went over all the rules, expectations, and when no one knew either of us, the selection process began. Many were disqualified as they had a reason they couldn't be on the case as a juror, from one pregnant lady due at any time, to scheduled surgery for another, and so on. After the last person was excused, we were given an hour lunch.

The afternoon was basically the same exact way as the morning had been, and we were finally able to narrow down the selection to six people, and two alternates, in case a juror could not continue for some reason. I had always thought there were twelve on a jury, but learned that was only for criminal cases. For my case, we needed only six, and five had to agree. After that was over, we were told our case would start at 9:00 am the next day.

I was exhausted by the time we got back to the hotel, and I hadn't done anything, but look at people, and help make the decision between Phillip's attorney and us, on which ones we decided to keep and which ones to excuse. We felt we had a pretty good jury selection.

Phillip sat through the selection of jurors with such a smug look on his face as if he had already found me guilty, and now was just going to make me suffer. Tommy said the jurors would be able to see his pompous arrogant attitude without much trouble, once he opened his mouth to answer questions.

I closed the drapes in my room, turned on the TV and lights, before I ordered dinner from room service. Once again, I slid the cart into Tommy's room when it arrived, so we could eat together, since he already had his meal brought in.

Tommy went over a few things with me, and nodded when I answered. He wanted everything to go as smoothly as possible, and felt he had his opening statement clear and precise. He felt he was as ready as he could ever be.

The next day at the courthouse, it went back and forth for hours with one question after another from Phillip's attorney, and then Tommy would cross exam them. One witness after another testified. Phillip's attorneys asked them each about the same questions, and when they were finished, Tommy would ask them his questions. Tommy kept it right on target, and kept it short. They seemed to all have the same arrogant attitude as Phillip. I only recognized a few of them myself. Some witnesses weren't even listed to be questioned, to which the judge allowed, and Tommy never objected to. Tommy said that was good because if we ever needed to add something for us that wasn't listed, like our "smoking gun", the judge would probably overrule Phillip's attorney's objection to adding that vital piece of information.

Tommy questioned Phillip, and it didn't fail that his attorneys objected to half of his questions. I was beginning to feel like the judge was biased. I felt like we were losing on everything. I couldn't believe the lies Phillip spewed out his mouth that the court heard, which didn't look good for me. How could he lie when he swore to tell the truth, and nothing but the truth? Once we were through for the day I was a nervous wreck. I glanced over towards Phillip where he smiled a cocky smile, and he blew me a kiss. What a jerk, and no one else seemed to have noticed when I looked around the courtroom.

Once Tommy and I were in our rooms, I let the anger loose complaining to him how manipulating Phillip was, and how he blew me that kiss. Tommy told me not to look at him when I didn't have to, so Phillip wouldn't be able to intimidate me again. That was going to be his intent throughout the whole ordeal. If he could unravel me in any way, he was going to.

The next day I was called to the witness stand where Phillip's attorney berated me over so many things I never expected to be asked, which I had to answer. I was humiliated with some questions I was forced to answer. Then the window breaking episode from me slamming the door only proved I had a temper, and his attorney wondered out loud if that was how I treated the clients, and poor little ole Phillip. I explained the window broke when I slammed my door shut, but I had…. And I was cut off from finishing my answer about the door being broken before. As soon as Tommy was up to question me, he asked about that window. I was confused, was he trying to make me out to have a bad temper as well? But Tommy allowed me to finish my statement, and then submitted as evidence the paper trail I had concerning that window for several months previous to it breaking, and it wasn't repaired per Phillip's decision not to have it fixed. So, it was just a matter of time before the window would have fallen out, and shattered onto the floor as it had. Tommy asked many questions that had been overlooked by Phillip's attorneys that I answered, and as I answered I looked at the jurors trying to see their reaction.

Their faces were hard to read, and I didn't know what to look for in body language, but they all sat there stiff, and rather looked bored out of their minds. Tommy had several people from the bank as my witnesses, and they were very good at answering each question, especially Elizabeth. She painted Phillip as evil as evil could get, making me work the long tedious hours on project after project. Several times the judge had her answers stricken from the record when questions were objected to. A plus for Phillip.

I went back to the hotel feeling pretty good that night though. I wanted to call Elizabeth so bad to thank her, but I couldn't talk about the case outside the courtroom. Tommy joined me in my room for dinner the next few nights. I did manage to sleep very well those nights some how, once I had fallen asleep.

The next day Phillip was back on the stand with more things to discredit me, and produced more witnesses whom I didn't know. They were pretty thick with Phillip, and made him sound like a saint. A saint in their eyes, wow, he had them buffaloed. I wondered how much he paid them to testify and lie, like they had. I didn't understand why they were even called to begin with. They didn't have anything to do with the bank, they were basically friends of Phillip's that he socialized with at the bar.

It was my turn once again to be on the witness stand, and I was feeling the eyes boring holes through me as I spoke. I was sure the jury didn't believe a word from me now. I countered every lie Phillip spoke on his turn, and a few on the witnesses he had. I was grasping straws by now, and my head was hurting from the headache I had.

In the afternoon Tommy was able to continue with Phillip bringing up about him threatening me at my house, that Phillip had denied ever happening. I didn't expect him to be honest, Phillip had no scruples at telling the truth. That flew out the door the minute the trial started, so I looked like a liar to everyone now, I was sure of that.

Then Tommy called for a witness on my behalf, it was one of the attorneys that was present when Phillip had threatened me at my home. I glanced over to Phillip, and he obviously recognized my witness, and was mad as hell. I could see him seething as he sat there having to listen, as my witness recounted that day. Phillip knew he was caught then, and I wondered how he was going to wiggle out of his lies now. Tommy had asked the witness what his profession was. When he said he was an attorney, Phillip immediately pulled one of his attorneys towards him, to speak to him quietly. I took in a deep breath, and calmly sat back in my chair, as Tommy questioned my witness at great length. I had forgotten about all of them being at the house when

Phillip had threatened me, but Tommy hadn't, and I was glad he remembered them. I looked at the jury members and saw many of them change their expressions, as they shifted in their seats.

When it came for Phillip's attorneys to ask their questions, they declined. Tommy called another attorney witness after he was through with the first one. The same questions were asked and answered, by this one. Again, Phillip's attorneys didn't have any questions for him.

When Tommy was done with his questions, and again, nothing asked by Phillip's attorney, he looked at the judge telling to him he had a few more attorneys and judges as witnesses waiting outside in the lobby that had witnessed Phillip spew his threats, but seeing that Phillip's attorneys weren't offering to question the first two, was it necessary to bring the others in to hear from them as well, and Tommy also said he had an affidavit signed from a judge who also witnessed the threats and assault, but wasn't able to appear because of a trial he was presiding over. Tommy asked the judge if the court would accept his affidavit. The judge replied under the circumstances, he would and ordered it to be put into the evidence after he and Phillip's council reviewed it. Of course Phillip's council objected, but the judge overruled them, and had Tommy read the affidavit to the court. I noticed the jurors were now sitting up looking as if they were digesting every word Tommy spoke.

Phillip and his attorneys were quietly talking among themselves as soon as my witness was excused. Phillip was probably shocked to learn those hick hunters at the house that day, were actually attorneys and judges.

The judge called Tommy and Phillip's attorneys, to his

bench to discuss why he allowed the affidavit to be entered in to evidence. The white noise he put over the speakers was definitely annoying, but I just kept my eyes fixated on the table in front of me until that noise stopped. I wanted to look at Phillip so bad to see his reaction, but didn't dare to.

The judge announced that my other witnesses wouldn't have to come before him, and declared that Phillip had indeed, threatened me. I could hear the jury members shift in their seats more with that statement.

Later Tommy told me Phillip didn't realize who they were until they were called to the witness stand stating what their profession was, and he didn't want any more to be called up to the stand.

The trial went back and forth for several days and it didn't look like it was accomplishing anything of importance. I sat there next to Tommy listening to everyone testify against me without showing any facial expression for the jurors to notice. Many times it was very difficult, but I managed to keep my composure.

The last day of the trial was when Tommy was going to prove I did those reports solely by myself, after Phillip's attorneys were done questioning Phillip. Tommy's turn, and I was waiting to see how Phillip was going to squirm now. Tommy asked Phillip on each and every report he held up presenting for everyone to see clearly while looking at Phillip, if they were his work and only his work. Phillip lied saying they certainly were when he looked them over. Tommy then asked if he could give each of the jurors a different copy, of his choosing, to look over which Phillip happily agreed to while brimming from ear to ear, and with his chest puffed out with pride. He must have felt pretty smug, and confident allowing the jurors read them.

Tommy randomly passed out different reports upon Phillip's approval to each juror, and asked for some time to allow the jurors to look them over. Tommy was granted ten minutes. I wondered if any of them would have noticed the encryption, but they apparently hadn't. Tommy asked Phillip once again if these were the reports he did himself, and he agreed that they were, once again.

Tommy asked if Phillip if the judge could have one as well, to look at. Phillip was more than happy for the judge to have one, stating he wanted the judge to see what kind of work had been done to make the reports as great as they are. Tommy allowed Phillip to pick the one he wanted the judge to read himself.

Phillip's attorneys objected to relevance of his line of questioning, as he was beginning to repeat himself. The judge wanted to hear why, and over ruled him quickly.

Tommy spoke calmly, and loud enough that he wanted to be sure that these reports were the ones in question, that I was to have stolen from him, and he was going to prove Phillip was not telling the truth. Again, another objection, and Tommy rephrased his statement.

Phillip was sitting so smug and arrogant, puffing his chest out as he continued to explain each and every report was his hard and time consuming work, where he had to research many nights to get the reports accurate. To be the quality they can see before them.

Once Phillip completed his well rehearsed speech, Tommy asked him why was it then that they held an encrypted message on each and every report. Phillip's look was of pure disdain towards me. Phillip assured everyone that I wasn't smart enough to encrypt any message. I could feel the eyes from the jurors boring a hole into me once again, and I was afraid to even look over towards them.

Phillip was excused from the stand, and as he walked past my table, he chuckled loud enough to make me uneasy. I was nervous now, but Tommy whispered "boom" as he squeezed my hand. Time for the smoking gun to be presented. I returned to the witness stand where Tommy only had a few questions for me this time, but Phillip's attorney was pounding me with them as fast as he could. I was shaking by the time Phillip's attorneys were done drilling me.

Tommy stood back up to rebuttal, and the fun was going to begin. I had to explain to the jury how, and what the encryption said, which was on every single report. I explained that the phrase is exactly the same on all reports, beginning with the very first letter on the report, and all they had to do was put the bold letters in order to see for themselves.

I never saw papers being flipped over as fast as the jurors were now doing, the judge included. Tommy had the phrase displayed on the overhead in the room, and I could see the jurors eyes getting wide as they searched each page. Phillip was in a heavy discussion with his attorneys, and I could see the rage building as his fist hit the table several times.

The judge had a copy in his hands, and was shaking his head as he looked for the letters. It was so obvious to the judge now, who also hadn't seen the message before either.

Once everyone calmed down, the judge called Tommy and Phillip's attorneys to the bench with that white noise put back on, but this time I was close enough to hear some of what was being said. It wasn't good for Phillip. Phillip's attorneys wanted the evidence thrown out of court, but the judge said no, because it was Phillip who brought all the reports in himself as discovery, and claiming they were products of his hard work. Tommy had just acted upon it, to prove Phillip wasn't telling the truth.

Once their meeting was over, I was excused from the stand. I went to sit next to Tommy. The next thing I heard was Phillip's rage, and fist hitting the table before the table was tipped over with papers scattering in the air, and all around the floor. The judge was banging his gavel several times ordering Phillip to get under control or be fined, and or, removed from the courtroom. Phillip was showing his true self now, and I was glad other people were there to witness it. It showed the jurors who was the real one with the temper, because it wasn't me.

The jurors were excused immediately, while the judge explained the next process to us. It was only a matter of minutes before the bailiff handed the judge a piece of paper. The jurors had made their decision already. I knew that usually meant the plaintiff won, and I was getting sick to my stomach. I wasn't sure I could handle the news if that was what it said.

The jurors filed back in, and the judge asked the foreman if they reached a verdict, which the foreman replied they had. The judge read the paper the verdict was written on, and gave it back to the bailiff to return to the foreman. After a few seconds the judge asked for the verdict, and the foreman read that they found the plaintiff to be guilty on all charges he brought against me.

I thought I was going to faint with that news. My eyes were filled with tears of happiness. Phillip was fuming mad, and started shouting things against the jurors, which the judge put a halt to immediately. The judge also reprimanded him for his outburst, and found him in contempt of court fining him, since he decided to yell at the jurors. I'm sure everyone now fully understood the threats Phillip had made against me.

The jury was excused leaving the room quickly. I was shaking like a leaf, but not from fear this time. Not only was I cleared of everything Phillip accused me of, but I received a nice hunk of money for our counter suit against Phillip. He had put me through a lot of heartache, headaches, loss of pride, and intimidated me to no end, he humiliated me, had stocked me, and defamed my character, on top of the assault.

Phillip was taken out of the room while the judge asked us stay for a few minutes before Tommy would be able to go back to thank the jurors. Then he looked at me, and asked me where I got the idea to encrypt my work. I replied my professor in college advised all of us to find a way to own our work, no matter what, and no matter how. He smiled saying he was very impressed with my reports, and how I proved my ownership of the work involved.

Tommy was excused to go back to meet with the jurors while I cleaned up the table we sat at, so when Tommy came back out we could leave. I didn't want to stick around for anything that could happen.

Once we got back to our rooms Tommy ordered our meals to be brought to his room. I took a shower, and by the time our meal arrived, I was ready to eat. It was a wonderful feeling to have my name restored, and I could now live my life without worry of Phillip being around. Tommy and I dined on steak and lobster, with a bottle of champagne to toast. We had a lot to celebrate, and I do mean we. I won my case against Phillip, and Tommy won his first case in court, over several high priced attorneys Phillip had hired to hang me out to dry. We fell asleep rather fast that night knowing our lives could now begin, Phillip free.

The next morning Tommy and I went out for breakfast with our attorney friends from Michigan, and Elizabeth, before we packed our luggage. Tommy had booked a flight out for us while I showered last night. He knew me so well knowing I didn't want to stick around New York City any longer than necessary.

The attorneys were impressed with Tommy, and told him so. Tommy thanked them, and they each said if he was looking for a place to work from, he would have a job with them any time. Two more of the attorneys had even gone on to becoming judges, and told Tommy not to just settle with his life. I knew that meant a lot to Tommy.

Elizabeth had to get back to her life as well, but we had a few minutes to ourselves, and she told me how happy she was, and her new job was wonderful. I was happy for her. And I knew then what a wonderful friend I had in her.

It was later that night when we were laying in bed, that I realized the extent of Tommy's love for me. Not only that he waited for me all these years to come back home, but he never gave up on loving me. These past few months have been rather turbulent to say the least, but he was there helping me through everything unconditionally. Tommy proved I was the one doing all those tedious reports for Phillip, and I finally got the credit for doing them. Phillip never gave me that recognition that I deserved, where Tommy set the record straight on that.

My case had taken Tommy out of his comfort zone,

by having him as my attorney through this ugly mess, and just maybe it will change his mind about opening his own firm in our town. I don't know for fact, but I'm sure he'd represent every client with every ounce of confidence he had in himself, as he had done for me.

People scoff at the thought of having someone in shinning armor to rescue them from whatever they are going through, but I know deep in my heart, I had mine with Tommy. With Tommy's help and hard work, I will leave New York City in the morning holding my head high this time. I was no longer "Lexi the Loser", I was the winner!

HOMECOMING

When we got back home to the resort, all our friends were there waiting for us, and congratulating Tommy for the outcome of the trial. I looked around seeing all the banners hung up, and food made for this homecoming. Aunt Sandy beamed from ear to ear when I finally saw her. I rushed over hugging her as tears of happiness fell from our eyes. My nightmare with Phillip was now over, and I can actually stop worrying, and stop looking over my shoulder. I can now finally get on with my life. I look forward to it, and forget about my New York nightmare. I always knew I was right and should win, but sometimes you can still lose, even if you are right. The not knowing what could happen can make your life come apart, like mine had. It was such a good feeling to have such a big win, and all that behind me now.

We partied until the wee hours of the morning. I was so tired by then, but I did not want to stop celebrating. I was so impressed with Tommy's outstanding performance during the trial, how he held it all together with a calm, and soothing tone throughout the duration. I told him he really was a great attorney, and should think about opening a small law firm right here in town. Just take on a few clients at a time, and see where it might go. He was going to think about it, and I believed he would.

The resort opened Memorial Day weekend right on time, and everything went smoothly the entire summer. Tommy and I were able to escape for a few hours every Sunday to enjoy the lake and activities, while Aunt Sandy handled everything at the resort. Sundays were usually quiet days there. People just wanted to be on the beach to relax as much as they could.

It was always a great time during the summer. Everyone that rented the cabins were so friendly. We developed more than friendships with many of them. We sometimes referred to them as our extended family. It felt more like a family reunion from one week to the next. It was rather hard seeing many of them leave on Saturday mornings. Many booked a reservation right then for the following year, and before we knew it, our place would be booked for the coming year.

Tommy was busy all day getting people checked in on jet ski rentals, and the boats we had for rent. I pitched in when it wasn't as busy in the office so Tommy could get a few minutes of down time. Aunt Sandy was the social butterfly with all the guests. She'd sit with several guests getting caught up with the family details from everyone. How she could keep things straight in her mind, I don't know, but she did.

It was on the last Friday night of the season when we had our last potluck under the pavilion for the year. Tommy was busy grilling the hamburgers, hot dogs, and kielbasa like a pro. I made sure the side dishes were kept full for our guests that Maria had prepared. Everyone was having such a great time. We did this the every Friday night throughout the summer, getting all the guests together for one last night of friendship.

Once the meal was over, and the band was getting ready to play, Aunt Sandy wanted to acknowledge everyone for such a wonderful week by thanking all the helpers she had throughout the day getting the evening ready. So many were just smiling with several people that had tears in their eyes. I acknowledge everyone there as well, hugging my aunt, and telling everyone what a wonderful person she was, and how she has been right there for me all my life.

Tommy approached us from the side chiming in how great Aunt Sandy has been to him as well, since he came to live there as a kid. She not only was his employer, but had been like a mother to him, that he didn't have while growing up. Once he was done saying all that, that he took my hand in his, telling the people how I have helped him as well, and how much he loved me. It suddenly got very quiet. I thought something had happened, but when I looked to Tommy he wasn't standing next to me any longer. He was down on one knee holding a blue velvet box with an engagement ring sparkling like a disco light on a dance floor, proposing marriage to me. I had to have had the most shocked look on my face as I promptly squeaked out a "yes", to which our guests started clapping and cheering for us, as Tommy kissed me.

I had not expected that at all, but apparently Aunt Sandy had, as Maria wheeled out a huge sheet cake to celebrate our engagement. Champagne was poured in fluted plastic glasses that were passed out to the adults, ginger ale to the kids, and a toast made by Aunt Sandy. Our friends had shown up to celebrate with us, making everything so extra special for Tommy and me.

It was the most incredible night for me, and I didn't want it to end. After all the guests left to go back to their cabins and our friends left, Tommy and I walked along the beach holding hands, stopping several times to enjoy the many kisses we shared. I knew then and there, I was going to make Tommy the best wife I could, and he would be the best husband ever. We got home and went to bed to the best night of making love ever.

We all were up early to see our guests off, before gathering all the linens to wash. I did the gathering of them, while Aunt Sandy started the washers. Most of the guest had already taken them off the beds, and had them waiting on the couch to be picked up. It went by rather quickly that way. Everything was washed, dried, and folded, to be put into storage until next season. One large task done, by the time we were ready to have dinner. Tommy insisted we go out to dinner to celebrate, and we didn't object to that idea. It was nice to be waited on for a change, and not have to worry about the resort for awhile. Aunt Sandy joined us as we all had a lot to celebrate this year.

Aunt Sandy asked if we thought about a date for our wedding, and I looked at Tommy replying, "the sooner the better as far as I was concerned." Tommy liked that idea himself. He wasn't going to take a chance of losing me again.

The plans started over dessert, and continued all the way into the night. Aunt Sandy was insisting on giving me the best wedding ever. I told her that wasn't necessary, but she insisted, with Tommy thanking her for it. I hugged her, and she was happy she'd be able to help me with the plans, as if I was the daughter she never had. Tommy was also like a son to her as well, since he lived there more than half his life. I knew my mother would be pleased with the plans, too.

It's strange how two different families can come together, for what ever reason in their lives, to becoming one solid family filled with unconditional love for each other. Aunt Sandy had actually taken both Tommy and myself, under her wing to guide, nurture, and she instilled great values in both us, when we were such a young age, doing the best way she could without hesitating. Tommy and I were fortunate she was there for us through thick and thin, of the life events that we had to face in the past, and now in the future.

After a few weeks of pillow talking at night, Tommy and I decided we wanted to get married in six weeks, if that was possible. It was a very pretty time of year in Michigan with all the colorful leaves on the trees, and no hot weather to deal with. We discussed the matter with Aunt Sandy over breakfast the next morning, and she was glad we had picked a day. Now we had to be sure everything would be available for us to make it happen on such a short notice.

By the end of the day, I had the church reserved, the reception hall reserved, the band reserved, and we talked to Maria for the catering, which she was more than happy to do for us. Maria also insisted on baking the cake, and ordering all the supplies we would need to make the reception flow easily for us. I asked Fred if he'd think about walking me down the isle, since I didn't have a father to be there. His hands started shaking like a leaf, and I saw tears forming in his eyes. He was more than happy to do it, thanking me as the tears rolled down his face. He said it would be an honor, and thanked me for asking him.

I couldn't think of anything else other than shopping for my gown. Two days later Aunt Sandy and I went to Saginaw for the day, to find the perfect gown I wanted. I had found one on the internet that I liked very much, but didn't know if it would look the same as in the picture, or on me, which was the most important thing, so we stopped at that bridal gown store first. It was a good thing we had stopped there first, because as soon as I saw it, I knew we didn't need to go anywhere else. My mind was set on that gown once I tried it on, looking at myself in the mirror. It was perfect in every way. I knew I could have had someone sew one for me, but every single homemade gown I have ever seen, always looked that way, homemade, and on the tacky side of the scale.

Aunt Sandy and I made a list of everything that needed to be ordered, placing a deposit, with the owner assuring us it would arrive within two weeks, giving us plenty of time for any possible alternations that might be needed. Aunt Sandy found herself a dress also while there as well, and we were able to bring it home with us that day.

Later that week, Tommy and I went to the stationary store to pick out, and order the invitations we decided on. They could be picked up in three days giving me plenty of time to address and mail them out, at a respectable time.

Over lunch, Tommy and I discussed who we wanted in our wedding party, and both agreed we really wanted our friends from the pool hall to be the ones. Both Tommy and I didn't have any siblings to ask, so it was the perfect choice.

That night when we went to play pool, we waited until everyone arrived, before we asked them all if they would be our wedding party. They were very happy to do it. It was hard to concentrate on playing pool after asking them, when all we had was the wedding on our minds.

However, once our pool games were done, and we had won against the other teams, we could relax to go over a few details of our wedding plans with the others. They had all been through a wedding before, and was giving us good advise on several things. The guys were mainly planning the bachelor party for Tommy, while we women decided a trip to Saginaw in the morning. We needed to shop for some nice gowns. They were all happy to be a part of our special day, and looked forward to it which made Tommy and me both happy.

So many things we needed to do before we would become husband and wife. Several nights Tommy and I laid in bed talking about how our lives are finally getting back to normal. Now making wedding plans, it became chaos once again, but this time in a good way. This time we were happy to have all the craziness happening.

Tommy asked where I thought we should go for our honeymoon, stipulating he was up to any place that I thought would be great. After a few minutes of thinking, I smiled up at him telling him the only place I could think of was Mackinac Island, the same place we talked about when we were teenagers of going to when we had talked about getting married. Tommy smiled that gorgeous smile of his, saying it was the perfect place for us to go to. With the honeymoon destination settled, I snuggled back into his arms falling asleep.

OUR WEDDING

Many relatives were staying at the resort, that came in from out of town for our wedding. It was nonstop chatter at the house trying to get everything and everyone, taken care of. Aunt Sandy did a great job helping me get everything ready for my big day, as well as taking care of everyones needs. Luckily, everyone was pitching in to help at the resort making things go more smoothly.

I went from having my hair done that morning right after breakfast, straight to the church to get ready. Aunt Sandy had brought my gown and other items, to the church while I had my hair done. I think she needed some time away from the chaos at the resort to gather her own thoughts. Once I had my make up done, I started to get ready, when all of a sudden, the butterflies in my stomach were taking over. I was overwhelmed with everything that has happened the past several months that I wasn't sure if this was all a dream, and I would be waking up to a disaster around the bend.

Lucky for me, my friends came in to see if they could help me in any way. Seeing the expression on my face they grew concerned immediately. Probably thought I was going to run out on Tommy again like I did before, leaving him with another broken heart. I assured them that wasn't going to happen. I knew this is what I wanted, to be his wife, but I was just overwhelmed with life in general at the moment. My mom wasn't there to see me on my most important day of my life. She should have been there with me, helping me, and enjoying every part of this with me. They completely understood I was just having a hard time dealing with a few things, and tried in every way, to comfort me for my loss. It wasn't until Aunt Sandy arrived, and told me my mom is there, she has never left my side, her spirit will always remain with me no matter what is happening, and she just knew my mom was beaming with happiness and pride for me. I needed that little pep talk. I knew my aunt was right, my mom has been, and always will be a part of my life, no matter what, or where I am.

As we gathered our bouquets of bright yellow and orange chrysanthemums, we looked in the huge mirror admiring how beautiful everyone looked. Their burgundy gowns with contrasting long stemmed flowers looked beautiful. I carried miniature chrysanthemums of the three colors, yellow, orange, burgundy, with the ivy, and baby's breath in my bouquet. My gown was of satin with thick embroidered design on top, and down the three quarter sleeves fitting me perfect in every way. We were ready to embark to the wedding procession on time.

The church was filled, Fred was waiting at the top of the stairs to walk me down the isle. Once the bridal march started, everyone stood to watch me make my way to Tommy. As soon as Tommy had seen me, he gave me the biggest smile, and had happiness written all over his face. My goodness, how handsome Tommy looked in his tux standing there waiting for me to walk down the isle to him. Everyone was there to witness Tommy and I exchange our vows to each other, where we became husband and wife.

Tommy and I had a beautiful wedding that October afternoon, in the church that had floor to vaulted ceiling stained glass windows overlooking Lake Huron. I couldn't have asked for a more beautiful day. The leaves were the most vivid colors clinging to the trees, sunny but brisk day, and the sky was a radiant blue like Tommy's eyes.

After we were pronounced husband and wife by the minister and kissed, I knew right then, my heart had been mended, and I was going to be fine. I may have taken the long road to get to this moment, but I was with the right person that I loved very much, and knew he loved me as well. It couldn't have turned out any better than what it has for us.

As Tommy and I climbed in the limousine to take us to the reception, Tommy pulled me onto his lap telling me how beautiful I was as he planted kisses all over my face. He couldn't have been any happier than he was right then. He promised me to always love me, and always make me the happiest wife he possibly could. I couldn't have asked for anyone better than what I have right before me now. My heart was bursting with love for him, and I will never have any doubts on it remaining that way.

The reception was absolutely fabulous. Aunt Sandy and Maria out did themselves with everything making this wonderful night possible. The table settings were absolutely beautiful, food was divine that Maria made, the cake was stunning, and what a fantastic band we had. Everyone seemed to be having a terrific time. We partied hard until it came time for us to leave for our honeymoon. We were staying the night at a motel in town, and start out in the morning for Mackinac Island. Aunt Sandy had packed a large tin of cookies and other desserts, telling us that we'd have something to eat when we came up for breath on our honeymoon, as she winked. Tommy thanked her taking the tins, and said he was glad to get the nourishment with her cookies, because he intended to keep me in bed all day long. That might be the only source of food to keep us alive during the honeymoon. First time Tommy had ever joked like that with Aunt Sandy. I know she thought it was funny, but her face turned red as well. I have never seen anything said by anyone before, that Aunt Sandy would be embarrassed from, but he got her this time.

Just as we were about to leave I saw Aunt Sandy at the end of the hall chewing someone out. I could tell she was really upset. I had never seen her so mad like this my entire life. She was spouting off to some guy who looked as if he was too drunk to realize she meant every word she saying to him. The guy wasn't happy about it, but he probably wouldn't remember any of it in the morning anyhow. Good grief, he could barely stand up on his own. I didn't recognize the man, but apparently Aunt Sandy knew who he was, and she was handling him pretty good on her own. It wasn't until the man staggered towards her, that she had Fred remove him from the building. The man swung at Fred, and soon found himself flat on the floor looking up at Fred. What the heck was going on?

Aunt Sandy saw us watching and quickly motioned to us with her hands, that everything was alright. Her smile she tried hard to show, didn't give me the impression that everything was alright. I had to know what was going on, and why that man was even here. All Aunt Sandy said was that he was not an invited guest, that he needed to leave, but he got ugly refusing to do so. That was when Fred stepped in. I don't think that guy knew not mess around when Fred was there. Fred was an extremely strong man, even at his age, and definitely not one to reckon with. There seems to always be that one person to cause a ruckus at a special event. He probably got drunk from our liquor too!

As long as everything was under control, Tommy and I left. We weren't going to let anything stop us from enjoying our honeymoon one more moment.

ℰPILOGUE

Shortly after we were married, Tommy opened a small office in town to represent people who needed an attorney, legal advise, or wills drawn up to help us through the slow months at the resort. He has been very successful helping people out with their dilemmas in our town, and he was appreciated for his skills, and quality of work he had provided. In time, his goal is to be open year round, but the resort is the bigger part of our lives until then.

Several years down the road our hunters started dwindling in numbers that came up for their week of hunting. On their last trip up, there were only four of them, and they mentioned one night that this was their last trip to hunt together. Their age was getting the better of them, thinking the adventure would pass down to their kids and grandkids, but the kids had absolutely no interest in hunting at all. So, they decided this hunt would be their last one, and they would put the land on the market to sell. Aunt Sandy felt bad for them because they had been doing their hunting on that property for over thirty years, and each time staying at her resort.

That night at dinner she told us that she had been thinking all day about them selling the property across the street when she came up with a great idea. With more families buying campers and motorhomes to stay in, instead of a cabin, she thought maybe she should invest some of her money into that property, and make it an RV Resort. Tommy thought it was a big step and with Aunt Sandy getting older, did she want to expand because of the work it would take and a great deal of an investment. Tommy said depending on her decision, he would be there to help with anything he could, including any legal work that would be needed.

Of course she liked that idea of Tommy helping her, and she would discuss the thought of buying it to the hunters in the morning before they left to go back home. There was enough acres there that would hold a lot spaces for the campers and motorhomes without people being on top of each other. The beach would be right across the street for them to enjoy, and we could provide them with a golf cart shuttle services to get them back and forth from the beach, so they wouldn't have to get across the busy highway on their own. Aunt Sandy was full of ideas once we started talking about it, and she couldn't wait to talk with the hunters about her ideas.

When Aunt Sandy talked to them the next day telling them some of her ideas, they were impressed and would get back with her when they talked with the rest of the hunters that owned part of the land. They didn't think the others would object to selling to her and they added they might want to come back to stay where they had made so many great memories.

It took about two day for the hunters to get back with Aunt Sandy stating they all agreed to sell the property to Aunt Sandy and gave her the asking price. They gave her a good deal on the price, and between all of the hunters and Tommy, they could have the papers drawn up in about two weeks. Aunt Sandy was more than excited to get the plans drawn up on the property putting water, electric, and sewer lines in, along with the concrete pads for the campers and motorhomes to park on. She thought she'd add a picnic table to every site for the campers to enjoy eating outside and a stationary fire pit that would be away from the vehicles but cozy enough to enjoy.

The very next summer we were in full service with the RV Resort by taking reservations early spring. We were still busy with the cabins as usual, but the additional choice to bring your own camper instead, made a new generation of people coming, we were at full occupancy by the time summer rolled around. Tommy manned the RV shuttle while I checked everyone in at the gate. Aunt Sandy was beaming from ear to ear each month from the earnings she had coming in. It also meant she had to hire a few other people, but she didn't mind. There were always young kids eager to have a summer job, and they were hard workers, too. Many returned year after year to work there even after they had left for college, and came home for the summer months. It definitely was something we hadn't planned, but it happened at the right time for us.

Aunt Sandy passed away ten years to the day that Tommy and I were married. She loved our four bundles of joy that we had in rapid time, while she was able to. Aunt Sandy doted on them so much they started calling her grandma, which I didn't mind. Aunt Sandy was ecstatic the first time TJ called her that, which brought her great joy, and many tears. Then Theresa, Timmy, and Tony followed his lead. They were such a blessing, but a handful all the same, being so close in age.

Aunt Sandy had left the resort to me in her will with hopes it continues to be as successful for us, as it had been for her. Maria had told me Aunt Sandy had made that decision once I came home for good from New York. It bothered Aunt Sandy that other family members would try to get their hands on it, and Aunt Sandy surely didn't want that to happen. Aunt Sandy's will was very detailed on her wishes, and had left a long letter for me personally.

I smiled and cried at the same time, as I read my letter from her. The love Aunt Sandy had for us was apparent, and her wishes of happiness for us, Tommy and me, and our kids, were apparent in her letter. We were her family, and she loved every minute being a part of it. I held that letter to my heart when I finished reading it. Tommy comforted me when I was done, telling me she was always thinking of me. Actually, she thought of us, because she helped raise Tommy as much as she did me.

I did learn who had turned Phillip in for his fraud. It was Fred, of all people! He was definitely not the one I thought had done it. I knew it hadn't been Aunt Sandy or Maria, but never thought about Fred. After Maria had told Fred what Phillip had done to his clients, how poorly his treatment of me, and that he was accusing me of being the snitch, Fred took it in his own hands to do what was right. Fred knew the right people to contact, to get Phillip where it hurt him the most, in his wallet. There was nothing Fred could do about what Phillip had done to me personally, but he could do something about the over charging he had done on his clients bills. It only took one phone call to get everything going against Phillip.

Never heard from Phillip again, and after several years I lost touch with Elizabeth. It was like I finally severed all ties with New York City, and I was fine with that. Heather had moved back home with her parents after Phillip fired her. She had their baby, a girl, and even though Phillip was never a part of her life again, Heather was able to collect child support from him while he was serving time for his fraud. No child visitation rights for Phillip when he'd get out either, which wasn't a big deal to him, he hated kids to begin with.

Aunt Sandy told me on her death bed that the man at our wedding that had caused such a horrible scene, was my birth father. He had read in the paper about my settlement from my case against Phillip, and planned to squeeze into my life to get some of that money for himself. He heard I was getting married, and planned to stop my happiness from happening. He drank so much he had lost track of where he was, until he saw I was getting ready to leave for our honeymoon. He never returned to Michigan from what Aunt Sandy knew. She felt bad that she had kept this from me, but she knew he wasn't up to any good, and she definitely didn't want him to ruin my special day. She didn't want to leave this life with that lingering on her mind, and to ask for my forgiveness in what she had done. She didn't need me to tell her she had done the right thing, as she closed her eyes for the last time.

THE END

About the Author

Joann Buie

Joann was born and raised in Ashtabula, Ohio, and liked writing short stories and numerous poems for others to read. Two hours after graduating from high school, she moved to Michigan to be with her husband, Bo, who was serving in the Air Force.

Moving to Arizona in 1979 as a young mother of three, Joann went to work in the school district in the Special Education department while completing her Bachelor's Degree. She earned her Master's Degree from Northern Arizona University while teaching elementary education.

After over twenty years working in the educational field and living over forty years in Arizona, she retired and now resides in Florida with her husband and two little dogs, Charlie Brown and Lucy.

Joann has been married for over fifty years, has three grown children and is a grandmother to seven.

Other Works

Abby's Quest

 Abby struggled with her life right from the beginning by living in one foster home after another, until she graduated from high school. Everyone had referred to her as the basket baby that had been abandoned at a fire station after her birth, which was difficult for her to overcome.

Knowing she wanted to escape from her hometown and her past, and make a fresh start with her life in another town or state, she accepted a house sitting job in Jasper, Tennessee, not knowing what to expect or what would be waiting for her around the corner.

Enjoy the heartwarming debut Abby's Quest from Joann Buie.